"Stayed in from recess to read it . . . **CAN'T WAIT FOR NEXT ONE!**"
—Zac A., age 9, Hood River, Ore.

"I like **COOL HEROES AND ROBOTS**—and Hilo is both!"
—Malcolm S., age 9, Riverdale, N.Y.

"**GINA WAS MY FAVORITE** character because she's into science and soccer like me! I also liked D.J.'s family because it looks like mine!"
—Kiran M., age 7, Carlsbad, Calif.

"*Hilo* is **REALLY, REALLY FUNNY.** It has a **LOT OF LAUGHS.** The raccoon is the funniest."
—Theo M., age 7, Miami, Fla.

"**HIGH ENERGY** and **HILARIOUS**!"
—Gene Luen Yang, National Ambassador for Young People's Literature

"**FANTASTIC. EVERY SINGLE THING ABOUT THIS . . . IS TERRIFIC.**"
—Boingboing.net

"My students are obsessed with this series. **OBSESSED!**"
—Colby Sharp, teacher, blogger, and co-founder of the Nerdy Book Club

"More **GIANT ROBOTIC ANTS** . . . than in the complete works of Jane Austen."
—Neil Gaiman, author of *Coraline*

"Anyone who loves to laugh should read *Hilo*. It is **ACTION-PACKED** with a robotic touch."
—Breslin S., age 10, Jackson, Mich.

"*Hilo* is loads of **SLAPSTICK FUN!**"
—Dan Santat, winner of the Caldecott Medal

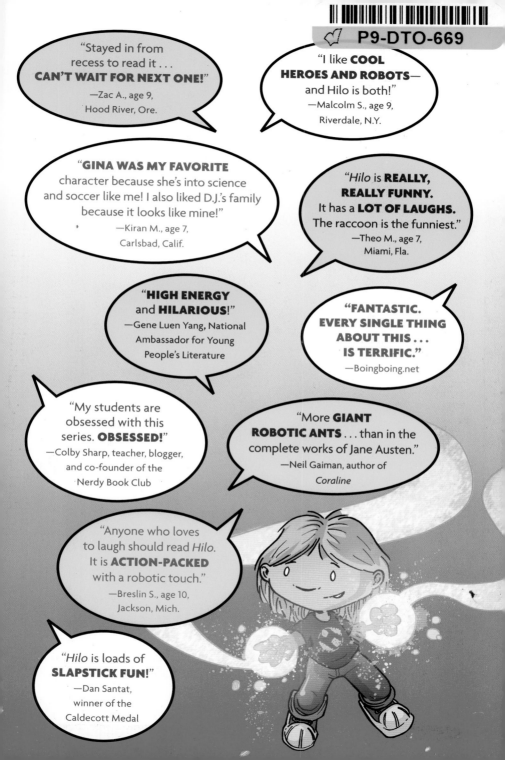

## READ ALL THE HILO BOOKS!

HILO #1 THE BOY WHO CRASHED TO EARTH

HILO #2 SAVING THE WHOLE WIDE WORLD

HILO #3 THE GREAT BIG BOOM

HILO #4 WAKING THE MONSTERS

HILO #5 THEN EVERYTHING WENT WRONG

BOOK 5

# THEN EVERYTHING WENT WRONG

## BY JUDD WINICK

COLOR BY
STEVE HAMAKER

RANDOM HOUSE NEW YORK

 Published in the United States by Random House Children's Books, a division of Penguin Random House LLC, New York.
Random House and the colophon are registered trademarks of Penguin Random House LLC.
Visit us on the Web! rhcbooks.com
Educators and librarians, for a variety of teaching tools, visit us at RHTeachersLibrarians.com
*Library of Congress Cataloging-in-Publication Data*
Names: Winick, Judd, author.
Title: Hilo. Book 5, Then everything went wrong / by Judd Winick.
Description: First edition. | New York : Random House, [2019] |
Summary: "As D.J., Gina, Hilo and Izzy go on another adventure together, Hilo gets even closer to answering the questions of his past. But the shocking answers he gets are not the ones he expected or wanted"—Provided by publisher.
Identifiers: LCCN 2017034073 | ISBN 978-1-5247-1496-3 (hardcover) |
ISBN 978-1-5247-1497-0 (hardcover library binding) | ISBN 978-1-5247-1498-7 (ebook)
Subjects: LCSH: Graphic novels. | CYAC: Graphic novels. | Robots—Fiction. | Friendship—Fiction. | Extraterrestrial beings—Fiction. | Identity—Fiction. | Science fiction.
Classification: PZ7.7.W57 Hm 2019 | DDC 741.5/973—dc23
Book design by Bob Bianchini
MANUFACTURED IN CHINA
10 9 8 7 6 5 4
First Edition

for

SHANA and JODI

who always
light
the way

# CHAPTER

# GOING TO BE HARD

D.J.!

THIS IS
**HILO.**

HE'S MY BEST FRIEND.

HE'S ALSO A ROBOT
FROM ANOTHER PLANET.

HE'S GOING TO SAVE ME.

HE'S GOING TO SAVE EVERYONE.

BUT FIRST HE HAS TO REMEMBER WHO HE REALLY IS.

AND THAT'S GOING TO BE **HARD.**

# CHAPTER 2

# HERE

DR. HORIZON.
HOW ARE --

WHUMP

YOU'RE HERE!
I'M HERE.

DID **IZZY** --
SHE SENT ME A MESSAGE --

YOU BUILT A **SHIP** --
THAT COULD TRAVEL IN THE VOID BETWEEN **OUR** WORLD AND **THIS** ONE.

AND IZZY OPENED PORTALS TO GET YOU HERE!
YEP.

YOU'RE HERE!
I'M HERE.
AND I --

WHUMP

YOU'RE HERE!
I'M HERE.

WHAT ARE THEY SAYING?

YOU CAN'T UNDERSTAND US. WE'RE TALKING

WHAT?

WHAT?

IT'S OUR LANGUAGE FROM OUR PLANET. HILO AND ME ARE ROBOTS. SO WE CAN ABSORB LANGUAGES FROM PEOPLE. DR. HORIZON CAN'T SO HE SPEAKS

OOH. YOU'RE NOT PRONOUNCING IT RIGHT.

YOU KIND OF SAID, "I HAVE A FROG BUTT."

WHICH I DO NOT.
**TOTALLY** DO NOT.
GUYS! WHAT ARE THEY SAYING?!

HERE! THESE **NANOBYTES** CAN TRANSLATE RIGHT INTO YOUR EARS.

**WHOA!** YOU'RE PUTTING TINY ROBOTS IN OUR **HEADS?!**
YEAH!
**TICKLES! TICKLES!!**

THERE'S **SO** MANY THINGS I DON'T REMEMBER.

**RAZORWARK** TAMPERED WITH YOUR MIND. HE MADE YOU FORGET.

HE'S COMING TO EARTH.

YES. THAT'S WHY IT'S SO IMPORTANT THAT YOU REMEMBER EVERYTHING **NOW.**

RAZORWARK WILL RAIN DOWN ON US ALL.
DOCTOR?!
IZZY!

HE'LL BE OKAY.

HE HAD TO TRAVEL THROUGH TWO PORTALS **AND** THAT CREEPY **VOID** BETWEEN OUR WORLD AND EARTH. AND THAT PLACE IS FULL OF ALL KINDS OF **WHACK-A-DOO** SPACE JUNK.

IT'S NOT HARD FOR ROBOTS, BUT **WAY** TOUGH FOR A REGULAR PERSON'S BODY. THAT'S WHY HE HAD TO MAKE THAT **SHIP** TO GET TO US. BUT IT GOT A LITTLE WRECKED FLYING HERE.

WHERE **IS** HIS SHIP?

I **TELEPORTED** IT INTO THE CAVE WITH ALL THE BUSTED-UP GIANT MONSTER ROBOTS.

WOOF!

HE JUST NEEDS TO REST. THIS **CRYO-CHAMBER** I MADE WILL HELP HIM HEAL.

HOW LONG WILL HE SLEEP?
TWO WEEKS, MAYBE THREE. WHEN HE WAKES UP, HE'S GOING TO HELP.

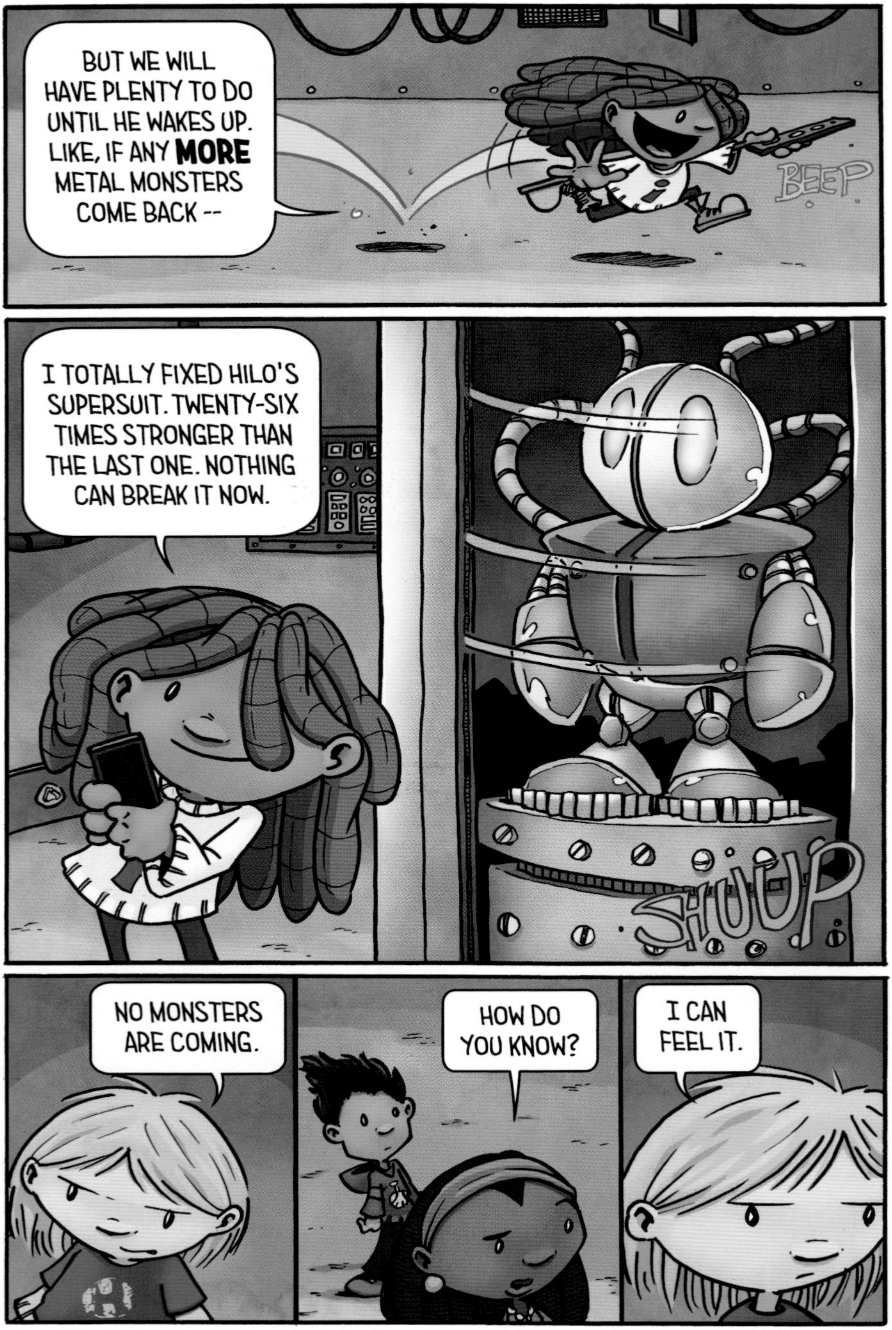

I TOTALLY FIXED HILO'S SUPERSUIT. TWENTY-SIX TIMES STRONGER THAN THE LAST ONE. NOTHING CAN BREAK IT NOW.

SHUUP

EVERYTHING IS GOING TO BE OKAY.

I MADE AN **OTTER** THAT CHIRPS WHEN EVERYTHING IS GOING TO BE OKAY.

CHEEP

EVERYTHING IS GOING TO BE OKAY.

ALL THE PIECES FIT.

# CHAPTER 3

# WHACK-A-DOO

FORT RISPLER MILITARY BASE.
DON'T TELL ME WE **CAN'T** FIND HIM...
TELL ME **HOW** WE ARE GOING TO FIND HIM.
IT'S PROVING TO BE DIFFICULT, SIR.
DIFFICULT?

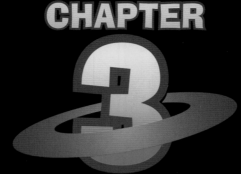

THE COMET -- WHO TURNS OUT TO BE A TEN-YEAR-OLD BOY -- WAS UNCONSCIOUS IN THE LABORATORY OF OUR SCIENTISTS -- WHO ARE SUPPOSED TO BE SOME OF THE SMARTEST EGGHEADS IN THE WORLD -- AND THEY DIDN'T EVEN GET A PHOTO OF HIM?!

IT'S BLURRY, BUT WE THINK WE **MIGHT** BE ABLE TO FIND A MATCH USING FACIAL RECOGNITION SOFTWARE.

THAT'S ASSUMING THAT HIS PHOTO IS IN **ANY** COMPUTER DATABASE. I MEAN, HE **LOOKS** LIKE A TEN-YEAR-OLD BOY -- THAT MEANS NO JOB, NO DRIVER'S LICENSE -- **NOTHING** THAT REQUIRES HIM TO HAVE HIS PHOTO TAKEN.

I DON'T EVEN KNOW WHERE TO BEGIN TO LOOK FOR HIM.

THEN IT'S SIMPLE.

LOOK EVERYWHERE.

FIND HIM.

I'VE BEEN WORKING ON IT AND IT TOOK SOME PRACTICE --

SHOW AND TELL
BUT NOW IT **TOTALLY** WORKS.

SO, WHEN I **ARMPIT FART --** IT ATTRACTS PIGEONS.

PARP PARP PARP PARP PARP PARP PARP

PARP PARP PARP PARP

IF I CUP MY HAND TOO MUCH, IT SOUNDS TOO HIGH AND THE PIGEONS DON'T COME.

PREEP PREEP PREEP
SEE?
TOO HIGH.

PARP PARP
PARP PARP
PARP PARP
IZZY. YOU PROMISED NOT TO ATTRACT ATTENTION.

YOU DIDN'T WANT ME TO MAKE ROBOTS. THIS IS ARMPIT FARTING.
PARP PARP PARP
PARP PARP PARP

I THINK IT'S GOING REALLY WELL.
PARP PARP PARP
PARP PARP PARP

MS. POTTER, MAY I PLEASE GO TO THE BATHROOM?
YES.

KING

WHOA.

WHEN I DO MY RIGHT ARMPIT I CAN CALL SEAGULLS.
HARRIET TUBMAN
VONNEGUT

HILO'S HOUSE.
BEEP

HOOOM

WHAT ARE YOU DOING?!

HILO, WHERE DOES THAT PORTAL GO?

HOME. **JANNUS.**

WHY ARE YOU GOING BACK TO YOUR PLANET?
DR. HORIZON IS **HERE.** HE'S GOING TO HELP YOU.

HE **IS** GOING TO HELP YOU.

HE'S NOT GOING TO WAKE UP FOR **WEEKS.** I HAVE TO ...

I NEED ANSWERS **NOW.** HE TOLD ME I HAD TO GET MY MEMORIES BACK RIGHT AWAY.

RAZORWARK IS COMING. HE WILL BE HERE SOON.
I JUST KNOW IF I GO BACK HOME, I'LL BE ABLE TO REMEMBER.

LET US GO WITH YOU.

NO. IT'S TOO DANGEROUS. I DON'T KNOW WHAT I'LL FIND. I'LL COME BACK -- I PROMISE.

WE CAN HELP.

NOT THIS TIME. I MEAN IT. I HAVE TO GO ALONE.

THIS IS JUST SOMETHING THAT I --

CLANG
CLANG

D.J.?
D.J.!
HEY! HE'S WEARING HILO'S SUPERSUIT!

COOM

D.J.!

HE SHOULD BE OKAY IN THE VOID. NOTHING CAN HURT THAT SUIT.

UNLESS HE FLIES INTO A STAR.
OR HITS AN ASTEROID.
OR GETS SQUASHED BY SOME BIG HONKING ALIEN WHACK-A-DOO.

ACTUALLY, HE COULD **TOTALLY** NOT BE OKAY IN THE VOID.

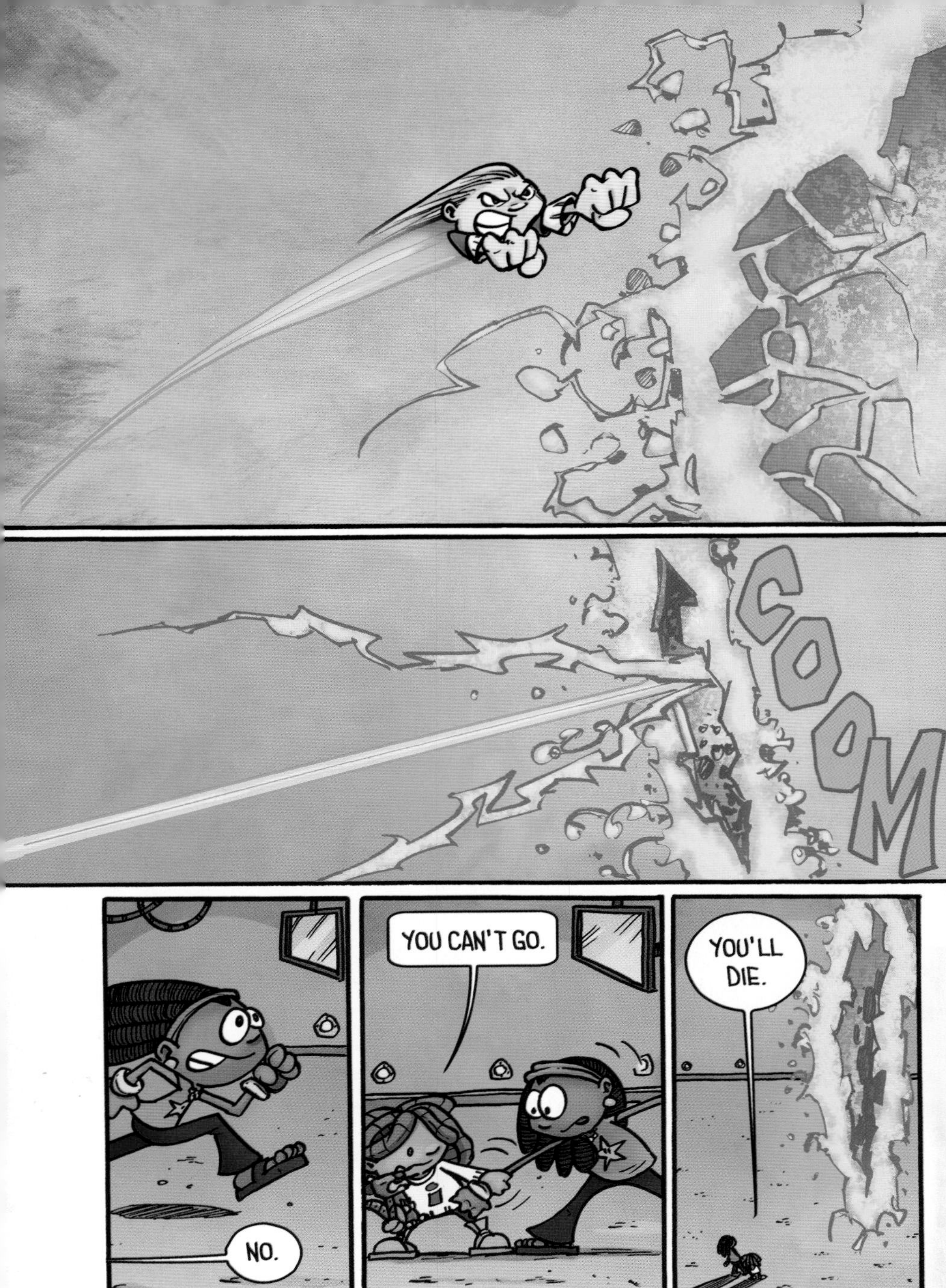
COOM
NO.
YOU CAN'T GO.
YOU'LL DIE.

DEEEEEEEEEEEEE-JAAAAAAAAAY!
WHOA.
LOOK OUT!
SPACE JUNK!
OW.
AAAH!
HOLY MACKEREL.
WHACK-A-DOO.

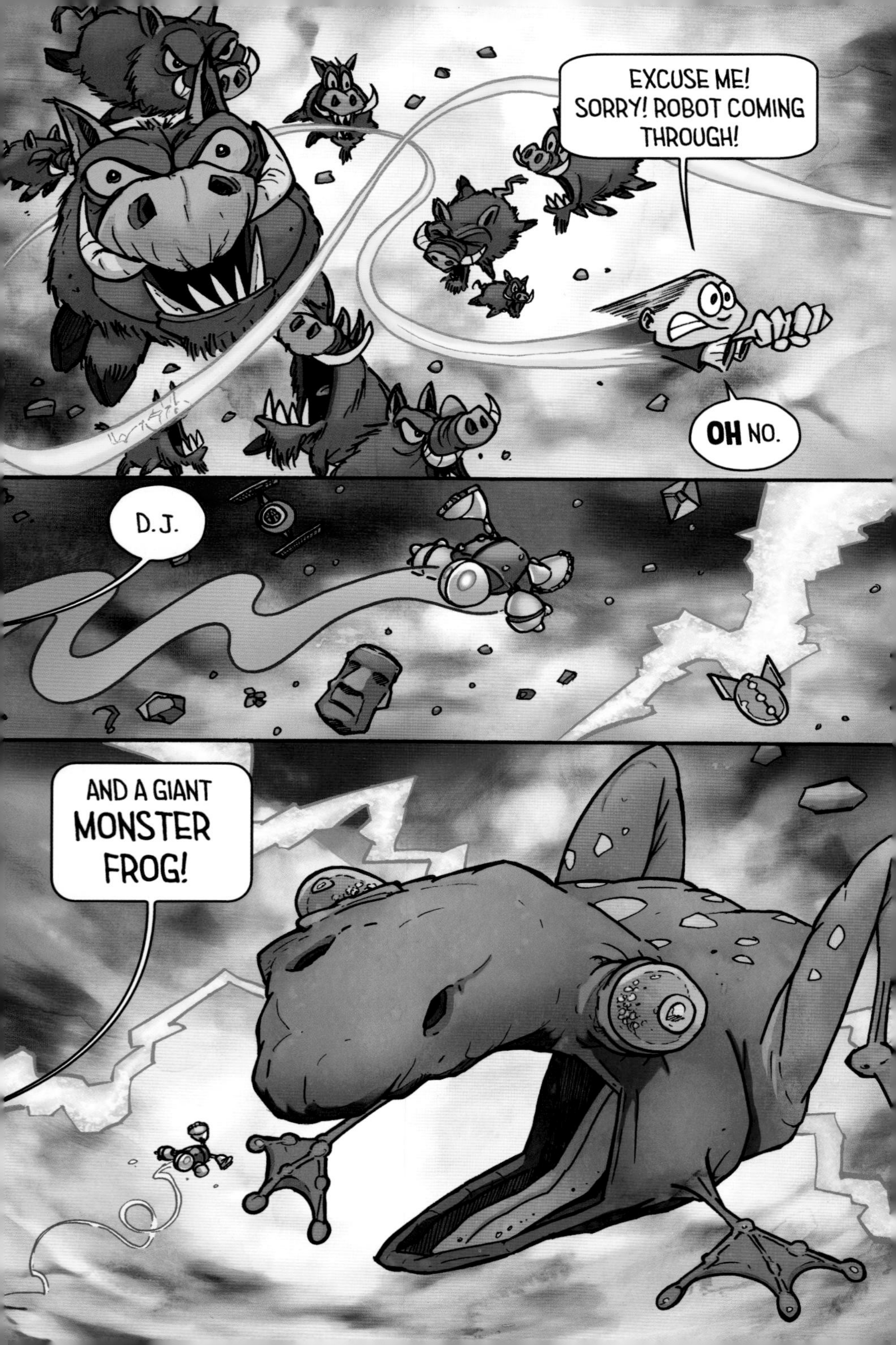
EXCUSE ME! SORRY! ROBOT COMING THROUGH!
OH NO.
D.J.
AND A GIANT MONSTER FROG!

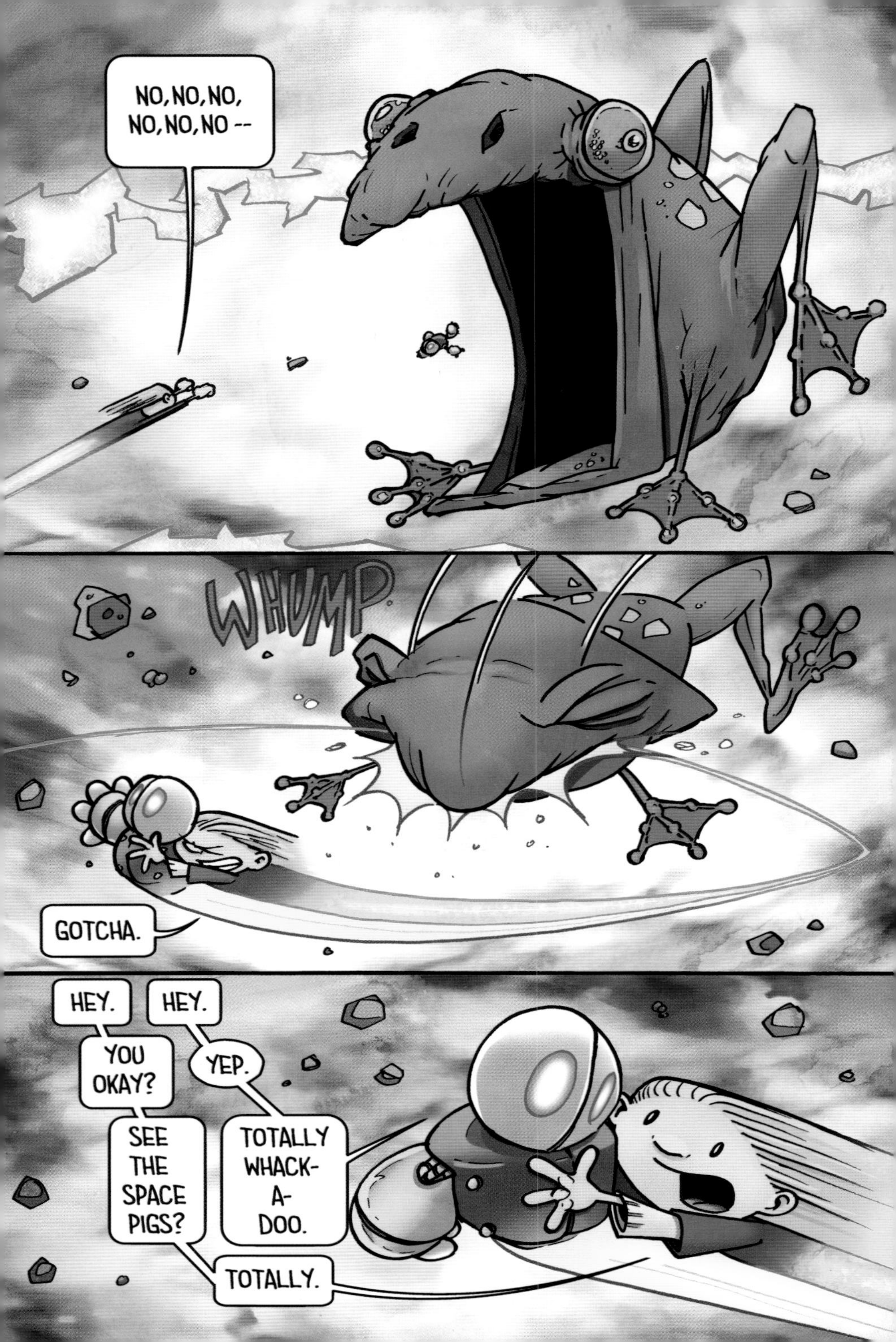
NO, NO, NO,
NO, NO, NO --
WHUMP
GOTCHA.
HEY.
HEY.
YOU OKAY?
YEP.
SEE THE SPACE PIGS?
TOTALLY WHACK-A-DOO.
TOTALLY.

WHY DID YOU DO THIS?!

I KNEW YOU WOULDN'T LET ME COME WITH YOU! SO I DIDN'T GIVE YOU A CHOICE!

AND I KNEW YOU'D SAVE ME.

WHACK-A-DOO.

BUT I'M GLAD YOU'RE HERE.

DOES THIS PLACE **ALWAYS** SMELL LIKE A **GORILLA'S ARMPIT?**
ALWAYS.

HWEEEEEEEE
WHOA.
YEAH. HANG ON!

I THINK WE'RE COMING UP TO OUR STOP!

YOU THINK?! YOU'RE NOT SURE?!
NOPE. BUT WE DON'T HAVE A LOT OF CHOICES!

THAT FROG IS STILL TRYING TO EAT US!

AAAAAAAAAAAAAAAAAAAAAAAAAAAAAAAAAAAAAAAAAAAAAAAAAAAAAAAAAA
THE GOOD NEWS IS WE WON'T BE SMELLING GORILLA ARMPIT ANYMORE.

HOOM
AT LEAST I DON'T THINK SO.

AAAAAAAAAAAAAAAAA

COOOOM

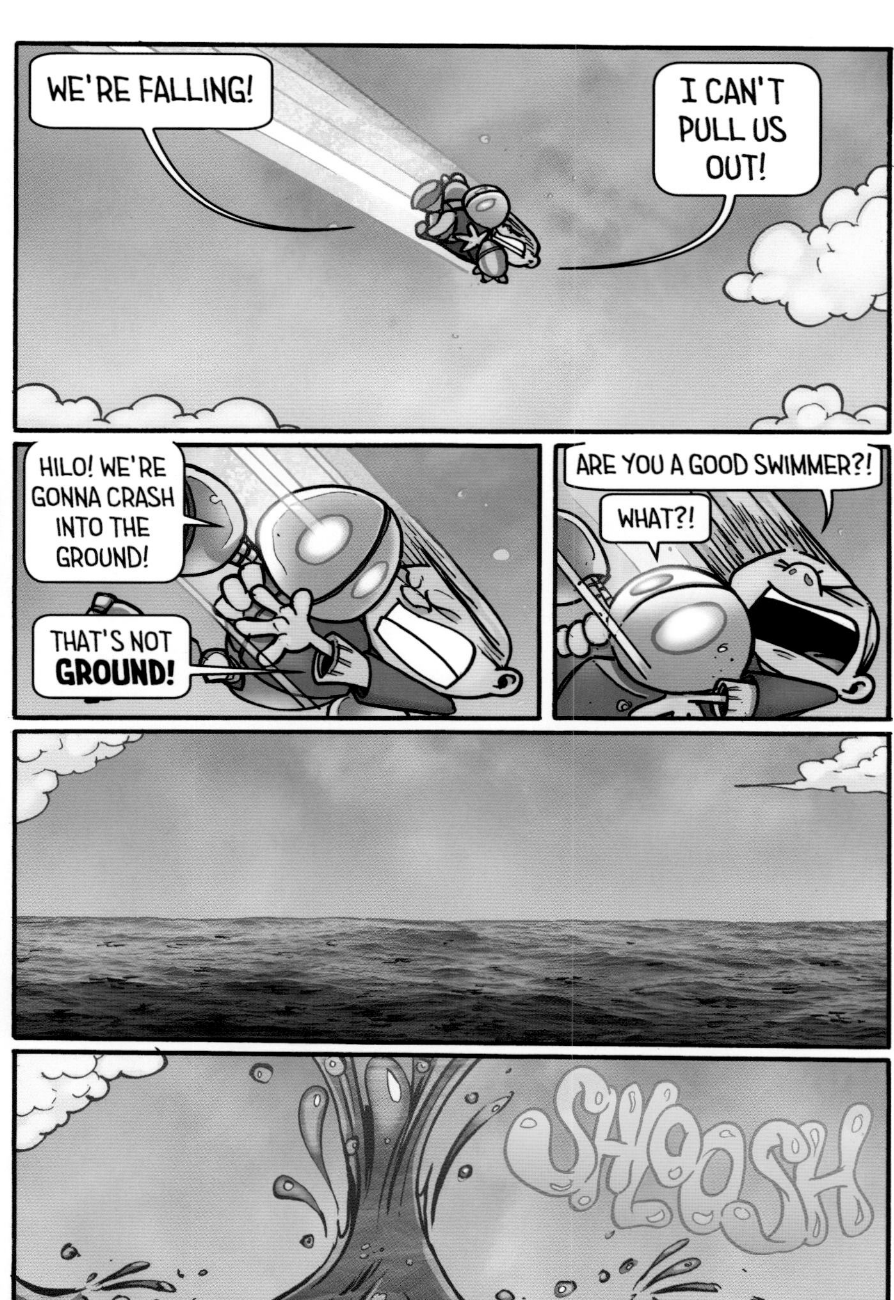
WE'RE FALLING!
I CAN'T PULL US OUT!
HILO! WE'RE GONNA CRASH INTO THE GROUND!
THAT'S NOT **GROUND!**
ARE YOU A GOOD SWIMMER?!
WHAT?!
SHLOOSH

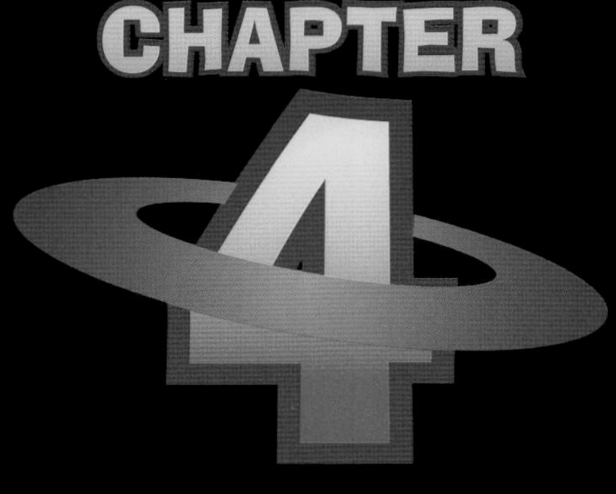


# CHAPTER 4

## BADA BOOM BA!

BUILD ME A SUPER-SUIT LIKE HILO'S!
IT TOOK ME THREE WEEKS.

WELL, LET'S FLY THERE IN DR. HORIZON'S SHIP!
IT'S ALL BUSTED UP. I CAN FIX IT, BUT IT'LL TAKE THREE WEEKS.

IT'S OKAY.
THEY'VE GOT EACH OTHER.

EVERYTHING IS GOING TO BE OKAY.

CHEEP

OH NO.

WE HAVE TO GO BACK TO SCHOOL.

YEAH. THIS IS A **LONG** TIME TO BE PRETENDING WE'RE IN THE BATHROOM.
NO -- IT'S NOT JUST THAT-- HILO AND D. J. ARE **GONE!** WE CAN'T JUST GO BACK WITHOUT THEM!

THEY'LL CALL D. J.'S PARENTS! THEY'LL CALL THE POLICE!

YOU **REALLY** CAN'T BUILD ME A SUPERSUIT?!
NO. BUT I CAN BUILD YOU SOMETHING ELSE.
CHEEP

NOW, CLASS...
VANDERBILT ELEMENTARY SCHOOL

IF YOU OPEN UP TO CHAPTER SIX OF YOUR SCIENCE BOOKS...

YOU CAN SEE WE WILL BE DISCUSSING INVERTEBRATES AND VERTEBRATES.

CAN ANYONE TELL ME THE DIFFERENCE BETWEEN --
HANG

OH YES -- D.J.
HANG

INVERTEBRATES DO NOT HAVE A BACKBONE. VERTEBRATES POSSESS AN ELABORATE INTERNAL SKELETON OF CARTILAGE AND BONE --
IN THERE

AND A SIGNIFICANTLY DEVELOPED BRAIN THAT IS ENCASED IN A SKULL. ALSO A NERVE CORD THAT IS ENCLOSED BY VERTEBRAE --
THERE

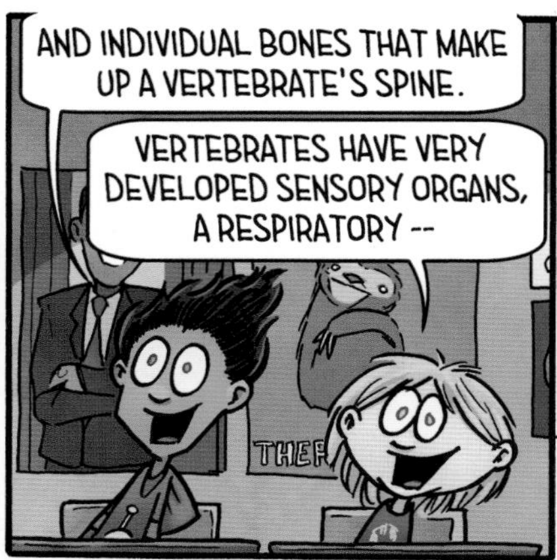
AND INDIVIDUAL BONES THAT MAKE UP A VERTEBRATE'S SPINE.
VERTEBRATES HAVE VERY DEVELOPED SENSORY ORGANS, A RESPIRATORY --

I THINK YOU MADE THE HILO AND D. J. ROBOTS A LITTLE TOO SMART.
YEAH?

AND A BILATERAL SYMMETRY WITH AN ADVANCED NERVOUS SYSTEM THAT FURTHER DISTINGUISHES THEM FROM OUR FRIENDS THE INVERTEBRATES!!

YEAH.

I MADE MY LUNCH INTO A MODEL OF SLIME GLANDS FROM A HAGFISH.

HILO'S HOUSE.
WHAT DO YOU MEAN?

WHAT'S WRONG WITH THEM?
SO MANY THINGS ARE WRONG WITH THEM!

I MEAN -- THEY LOOK EXACTLY LIKE THEM, AND THAT'S AMAZING, BUT--

I CAN SHOOT NICKELS FROM MY BELLY BUTTON!

POONT
TIIIIIIIING
OUTSTANDING!
HOW FAR CAN YOU SHOOT A CERAMIC FISH?

THEY'RE WEIRD! AND TOO BRAINY! AND THE HILO ROBOT SMELLS LIKE MANGO.
HILO LIKES MANGO.
MANGO!
POONT!

I **KNOW!** BUT HILO ISN'T ALL **STINKY** FROM MANGO. AND THIS D. J. ROBOT HAS TO GO HOME IN HALF AN HOUR! HE CAN'T BE ALL--

BADA BOOM BA!

WHY?
**THAT!** HE CAN'T BE ALL THAT!

IF PEOPLE -- TEACHERS, PARENTS, THE **ARMY** -- FIND OUT THAT THEY AREN'T HUMAN, THEY'RE GOING TO FIND OUT **EVERYTHING!** PEOPLE HAVE TO THINK THEY'RE **NORMAL.** THEY CAN'T BE THIS WEIRD.
POOMF

THEY CAN'T BE LIKE ME.

**IZZY.** YOU ARE ONE OF THE MOST AMAZING PEOPLE I'VE EVER MET IN MY LIFE.
YOU SEE THE WORLD LIKE **NO ONE** ELSE.
YOU MAKE **IMPOSSIBLE** THINGS **REAL.**

BUT WE HAVE TO BE CAREFUL.

OKAY.

AND THANKS FOR CALLING ME **PEOPLE.**

I'LL MAKE SOME ADJUSTMENTS.
**MANGO!**

I'LL MAKE SOME ADJUSTMENTS TOO.

TZEET

TZOT

WHAT ARE YOU DOING?

I'M GOING TO TRY TO BRING THEM BACK.
OR AT LEAST TALK TO THEM. I NEED TO HELP.
THIS IS GINA...
COME BACK...
OR...LET ME HELP...
HELP...
HELP...
HELP...
LET ME HELP...
HELP.
HELP.

BOOM
YOU DID IT!
NO. I'M NOT SURE WHAT I DID.
BLOOOCK
BLAM

GRRRRRRRRRRRR

AAAH!
NEAT. IS THAT WHAT'S SUPPOSED TO HAPPEN?

RAAAAAAAAGH

CACK
HUNK
AAAH!

OVER HERE.
I'M OKAY.

YOU'RE
OKAY?!
I'M OKAY.

I THOUGHT I PULLED
YOUR FEET OFF!
NO.
I'M
OKAY.

WHERE
ARE
WE?
ONE SUN. ONE DAY
MOON. AN OCEAN
THAT SMELLS
LIKE BANANAS.
THIS IS MY PLANET.

THIS IS
**JANNUS.**

WHAT'S THAT?

IT LOOKS LIKE IT'S **A CITY.** OR IT USED TO BE...

PEOPLE USED TO CALL IT THE **HEART** OF JANNUS.

THAT WAS MY HOME. THAT WAS **FARALON.**

ARE WE GOING THERE?
NO.
I FOUGHT RAZORWARK, AND HE DESTROYED IT.

WE'RE NOT GOING THERE.

THERE'S NOTHING LEFT.

# CHAPTER 5

# DOGS AND CATS

AAAAAAAAAAAAAAAAAAAAAAAAAAAA

ROWF
ROWF
ROWF
ROWF

YOU REALLY CAN'T STOP THEM WITH **MAGIC?**
I'LL TRY AGAIN!!
HOOM

TZOT

ROWF
ROWF
ROWF
ROWF
TZEET
TZEET

MY SPELLS DON'T WORK ON THEM!
I MADE A **TRANSLATOR** SO WE CAN UNDERSTAND WHAT THE DOGS ARE TRYING TO SAY TO US!

WHAT ARE THEY SAYING?
"BITE YOU! BITE YOU! I'M GOING TO BITE YOU!"

I THINK THEY WANT TO BITE US.
I GOT THAT.

ROOOWF

AAH!

CRASH

ROWF

BOOM

TZEET

CWOON

WEEEEEN

TZOT
CWEEK
TSSSSSST
WHUMP

NEAT.

WHO ARE YOU? WHY ...
WHY DID YOU HELP US?

I WOULDN'T THINK IT WOULD BE **TOO** SURPRISING.

I THOUGHT ON **THIS** WORLD ...

CATS DON'T
LIKE DOGS.

HILO...
RAZORWARK WASN'T ALWAYS BAD.
WHAT?
I **KNOW** YOU REMEMBER. **IZZY** SHOWED ME.
**RAZORWARK** WASN'T ALWAYS BAD.
HE USED TO SAVE PEOPLE. USED TO PROTECT THEM. THEY CREATED HIM TO BE A HERO.
THEN THEY MADE HIM FIGHT WARS.
THEY MADE HIM DESTROY OTHER ROBOTS.
DOING THAT... CHANGED HIM.
HE WASN'T ALWAYS BAD.

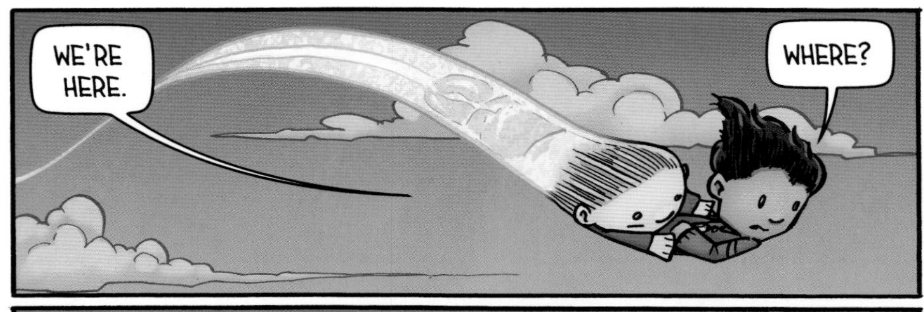
WE'RE HERE.
WHERE?

**CATADON.** IT'S ANOTHER CITY. BUT...
SOMETHING'S WRONG.

THERE'S NOTHING FLYING AROUND EXCEPT **US.**
WHAT? LIKE HELICOPTERS?

YEAH. LIKE FANCY SUPER-DUPER FAST HELICOPTERS, BLIMPS, CARS, BUSES -- ALL WHIPPING AROUND HERE. JANNUS IS A **MUCH** MORE TECHNOLOGICALLY ADVANCED PLANET THAN EARTH. CATADON SHOULD BE ...

ADVANCED.

AND WHERE ARE THEY?

WHO?

THE **ROBOTS.**

THERE SHOULD BE ROBOTS ... **EVERYWHERE.**

HILO'S HOUSE.
WHAT AM I DOING HERE?!

YOU GAVE ME A **SHOUT** AND I CAME **RUNNING!**
A SHOUT?

**AYE!** LOOK AT YOU! SENDING COMMUNICATION SPELLS ACROSS **DIMENSIONS!** YOU'RE STILL SPORTING MAGIC!

THAT MAKES ME SO PROUD, I COULD SPIT.

POON'T

WELL, I WASN'T **TRYING** TO CALL YOU, I WAS TRYING TO CALL HILO AND D.J.
DOESN'T MATTER! YOU MISSED THE TARGET, BUT YOU HIT THE TREE!

I WAS CHASING OFF **THESE** HUMONGOUS BAGS OF HAIR --

WHO ARE TREADING ON THE TERRITORY OF THE FURBACK CLAN!

WHEN I GOT YOUR CALL FOR HELP! A PORTAL OPENED -- THESE WARGIES SCUTTLED THROUGH THE DOOR BEFORE ME.

MY MAGIC WON'T WORK ON THEM.
AYE. THESE PUPS ARE MADE OF TOUGH STUFF. A HIGHER-LEVEL NECROMANCER -- LIKE MYSELF -- IS NEEDED TO KNOCK 'EM ON THEIR HINDERS.

BUT YOU FENDED 'EM OFF! SO! PROUD!

HAZZAH!
POOONK

ONE EXPLANATION OF WHO IZZY IS LATER...

I HOPE IT BRINGS YA SOME CHEER TO KNOW THAT WITHOUT ANY WEAPONS, THOSE PAILS OF LIZARD POOP ARE AS WEAK AS DRIED LEAVES NOW!

NOT REALLY.

WE ARE **BOUND,** GINA COOPER!

MY CLAN HAS LEARNED THAT EARTH, MY WORLD OF **OSHUN,** AND HILO'S PLANET ARE **LINKED!**

A **TRINITY!** THREES ARE **VERY** POWERFUL IN MAGIC.

LIKE HILO, GINA, AND D. J.

INDEED.

**AAAH!**

**AAAH!**
I LOVE THAT GREETING!

WHY IS D.J. A ROBOT, AND WHERE IS THE REAL HILO?
BRIIIIING
TELEPHONE.

OH. FOR ME?
I MADE THAT IGUANA. IT ANSWERS THE PHONE.
**OUTSTANDING!** WHAT'S A PHONE?

YES! **SURE!** YEP! I'LL TELL HIM! **THANKS!**

OKAY. SMALL PROBLEM.

D.J. HAS TO GO HOME FOR DINNER.

**AAAH!**
I COULD EAT.

POLLY, PLEASE, YOU SHOULD STAY HERE. LET ME HANDLE D. J.'S HOUSE ON MY OWN.
GINA, YOU'VE GOT THE FAKE D. J. AND THE FAKE HILO TO WRANGLE. YOU NEED SOME EXTRA PAWS.

EXACTLY! **PAWS!** YOU'RE A CAT! D. J.'S FAMILY WILL NOTICE THAT! WE DON'T HAVE TALKING MAGICAL CATS HERE ON EARTH!

I **KNOW.** I'M NOT COMPLETELY **DIM.** I'M GOING TO WHIP UP A MASKING SPELL.

A WHAT?
**A MASKING SPELL.** IT'LL CHANGE MY APPEARANCE. I'LL LOOK HUMAN.

NOW, I'VE NEVER MASKED MYSELF INTO ONE OF YOU HAIRLESS APES. I LOVE YOU BUNCHES, BUT YOU ARE ANYTHING BUT PRETTY.

BREEEEN
POOF

GOOD GRAVY.

I'M GORGEOUS!

YOU LOOK NICE.
NICE?! PLEASE, LOOK AT ME! I'M A VISION!

OKAY! LET'S GO MEET THE NEIGHBORS!
YOU STILL HAVE A TAIL!
I'LL FIX IT ON THE WAY OVER!

I CAN SHOOT NICKELS OUT OF MY BELLY BUTTON!
OUTSTANDING!
WHAT'S A NICKEL?

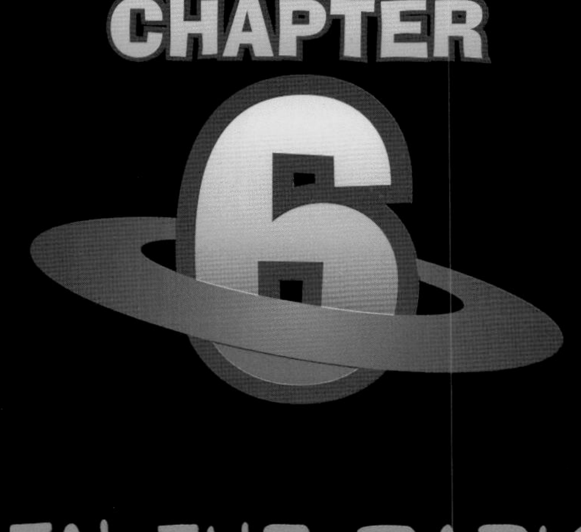


# IN THE DARK

WHAT DO YOU MEAN, "THE TECH IS GONE"?

THE TECHNOLOGY IS **GONE.**

**LOOK AT THIS PLACE!**

THE STREETS USED TO BE **FILLED** WITH COMPUTERIZED CARS AND GIANT METAL SPIDERS.
SPIDERS?

YEAH. BUT NICE SPIDERS. THEY SOLD SODA.
SODA SPIDERS?
YEAH.

COOL!
I KNOW!

BUT NOW THEY'RE GONE! NOW IT'S GOT FOLKS RIDING BIKES. OR ANIMALS. NO MACHINES, NO COMPUTERS . . .

NO ROBOTS.

IT'S LIKE SOMEONE TURNED IT ALL OFF.

C'MON! I JUST REMEMBERED SOMETHING.
WHA --

AAAAAAAAH!

WHY ARE WE FLYING THROUGH **ALLEYS?!**
I DON'T WANT ANYONE TO SEE US. I'M PRETTY SURE --

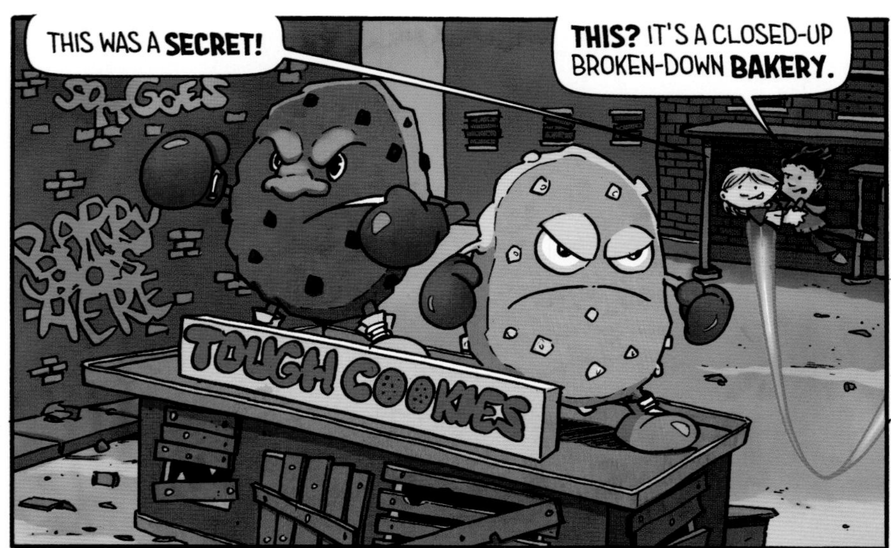
THIS WAS A **SECRET!**
**THIS?** IT'S A CLOSED-UP BROKEN-DOWN **BAKERY.**
SO IT GOES
BOBBY WAS HERE
TOUGH COOKIES

**YEAH.** GET IN THE NOSE.
WHAT?

**HEY!**
POONT

**HEY!**

AAA--

AAAAA--

WHUMP
WHOA.
YEAH.
WHERE ARE WE?

DR. HORIZON'S SECRET LAB.

HE HAD A LABORATORY IN EVERY MAJOR CITY. ALWAYS TRYING TO STAY A STEP AHEAD OF **RAZORWARK.**

SOMETHING'S HAPPENED. IT'S LIKE THE WORLD HAS TAKEN A HUGE STEP **BACKWARD.** DR. HORIZON'S COMPUTERS MIGHT HAVE SOME ANSWERS.

WAIT, WAIT. HOW CAN YOU SEARCH THE COMPUTERS IF THERE'S NO POWER?

PLUC
PLUC

BREEEEEEEE

BREEEEN

LOSS OF ENERGY --
OUTAGES ACROSS THE CITY --
BLACKOUTS --

REPORTS IN MOST MAJOR CITIES OF INCREASING POWER OUTAGES. THOUSANDS HAVE BEEN LITERALLY LEFT IN THE DARK --

OVER A THOUSAND CITIES --
MILLIONS WITH NO LIGHT, NO POWER --
A WORLDWIDE POWER BLACKOUT --

WITH ALMOST NO POWER REMAINING, TONIGHT WILL BE OUR LAST BROADCAST. WHY OR HOW THIS IS HAPPENING IS STILL UNKNOWN ...

**JANNUS** IS A WORLD THAT WILL HAVE TO **START OVER.**

THAT'S IT?
BWOOP

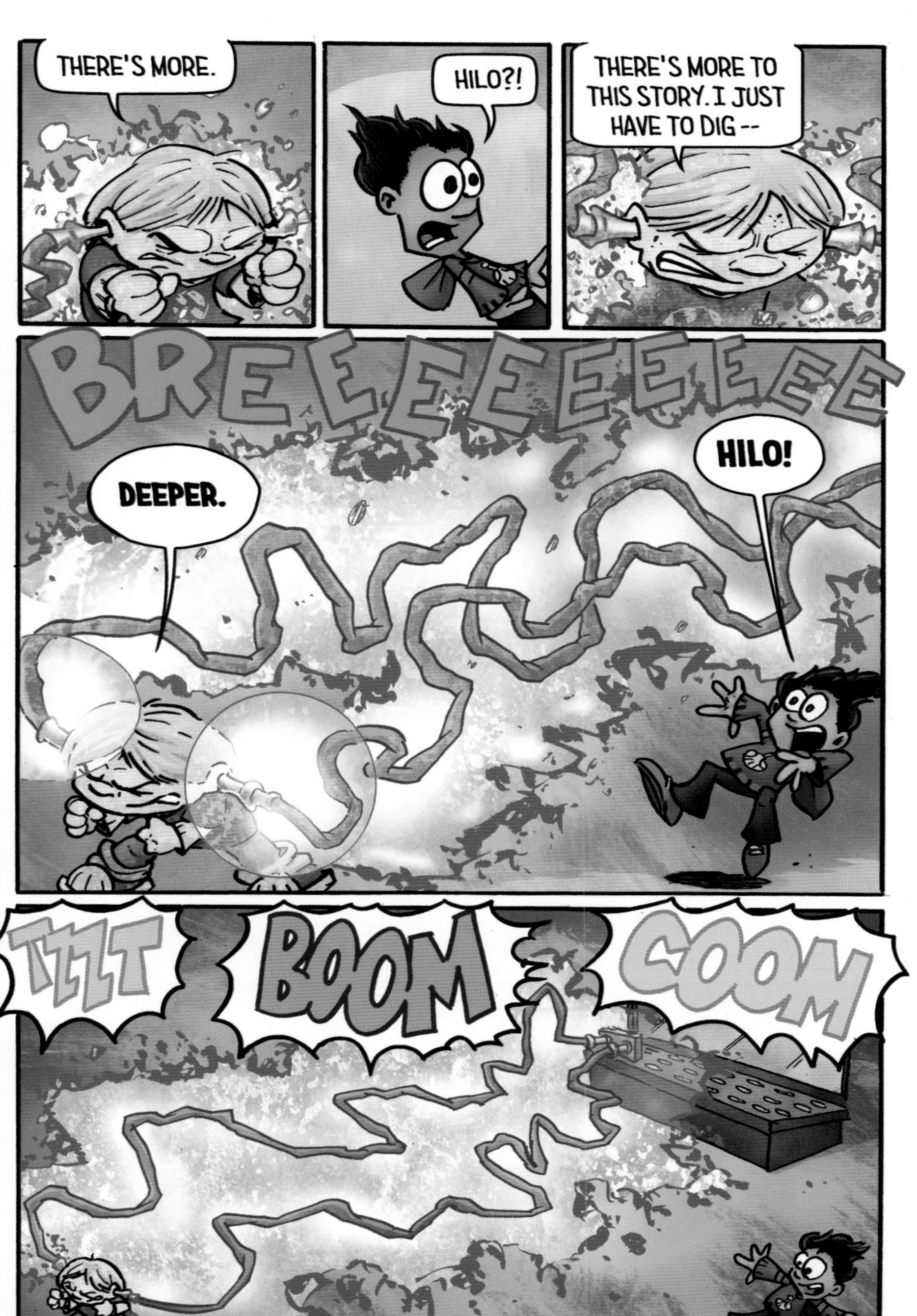
THERE'S MORE.
HILO?!
THERE'S MORE TO THIS STORY. I JUST HAVE TO DIG --
BREEEEEEEE
DEEPER.
HILO!
TZZT
BOOM
COOM

THERE'S MORE.
CREEEEEEEEE
TOK
TOK
HOOOOOOOooo
PLECK
PLECK
WHUMP
YOU OKAY?! YOU OKAY?!
I'M ... OKAY.

WHY?! WHY DO YOU ALWAYS DO THAT?!

YOU PUSH AND PUSH AND PUSH YOURSELF UNTIL YOU MIGHT GET DESTROYED!

I KNEW YOU'D SAVE ME.

BOOPOOP
DEEP

ZZZ
ZZ
ZZ
ZZ
RIGHT.
ZZ
ZZ
ZZ
ZZ

YOU'VE RUN YOURSELF OUT OF POWER.

SLEEP.

HERE ON ANOTHER PLANET.

IN A SECRET LAB.

I HOPE IT'S GOT A SECRET BATHROOM.

BECAUSE I **REALLY** NEED TO PEE.

EARTH. SECTOR E HEADQUARTERS.
C'MON ...

C'MON ...
SEARCHING

C'MON, C'MON, C'MON ...

COMPLETE
NO MATCHES FOUND
BEEP

AAH!
DANG IT! DANG IT! **DANG IT!**
MAN!

DO YOU LIKE PENGUINS?
SIR?

PENGUINS. DO ALL OF YOU LIKE PENGUINS?

I GUESS.
SURE.
I CAN LEARN TO LIKE PENGUINS.

GOOD, GOOD ... BECAUSE I'M THINKING OF REASSIGNING YOU ALL--

TO THE SOUTH POLE!!

WHERE THERE'S LOTS OF PENGUINS.
WHERE THERE'S LOTS OF PENGUINS!!

SIR, WE ARE LOOKING FOR **THE COMET** VERY HARD.
WE HAVE SEARCHED **EVERY** IMAGE DATABASE TO FIND A MATCH FOR THE PICTURE WE HAVE --
WE SEARCHED OVER **8 MILLION** PHOTOS!

THERE'S A VERY STRONG POSSIBILITY THAT THERE ISN'T A PHOTO OF HIM ON FILE . . . **ANYWHERE.**

**PENGUINS!**

I'M RAISING THE SEARCH FOR THE COMET TO **LEVEL FIVE.**
**FIVE,** SIR? THAT'S --

A SEARCH OF EVERY PRIVATE PERSONAL COMPUTER, MEDICAL RECORD, SECURITY CAMERA, SCHOOLS --

CHECK **EVERY** FILE AND COMPUTER DATABASE ON **EARTH?**

THIS "BOY" FLIES, FIRES LASERS FROM HIS HANDS, AND -- OH YEAH --

TOOK DOWN **DOZENS** OF 100-FOOT-TALL KILLING MACHINES BY **HIMSELF.**

HE'S AN ENTIRE **ARMY** IN SHORT PANTS.
WE'VE NEVER SEEN **ANYTHING** MORE DANGEROUS . . .

THAN HIM.
THIS IS **SO** OUTSTANDING!

YES! MOTHER, THIS IS ABSOLUTELY DELICIOUS!
DEE-LICIOUS!

ARE YOU USING MORE GINGER IN THE CURRY, MOM? BECAUSE I AM **REALLY** ENJOYING IT.
MORE MILK, DEXTER?
MILK

GLUB
GLUB
GLUB
MILK

WHAT'S UP WITH YOU GUYS?
YEAH. YOU'RE ALL KINDS OF CRAZY POLITE TONIGHT.

**TOTALLY.** KISSING UP **THIS** MUCH USUALLY MEANS YOU DID SOMETHING WRONG. YOU BOMB A TEST, D. J.?

I CERTAINLY DID NOT, DEXTER. IN TRUTH I HAD A MOST ENLIGHTENING DAY AT SCHOOL TODAY.

MOM! D. J.'S BEING WEIRD! AND HILO! I MEAN, HILO IS ALWAYS WEIRD, BUT THIS IS A **NEW** WEIRD.

IT IS.

I DON'T SEE THE PROBLEM IN USING GOOD MANNERS.

CAN I HELP YOU WITH THAT, MRS. LIM?
THANK YOU.

I THINK THE REPROGRAMMING WORKED. ROBOT D. J. AND FAKE HILO ARE ACTING MORE NORMAL.
WELL, "NORMAL" WOULDN'T BE THE WORD I'D USE.

I DO HAVE TO AGREE, MRS. LIM. NO SHAME IN A **WEE** BIT OF KINDNESS AT MEALTIME. AT SUPPER AT **MY** HOUSE WE'RE ALL PULLING **WHISKERS** AND **CASTING SPELLS**.

POLLY.
**FIGHTING!** BOATLOADS OF FIGHTING! WITH OUR **HANDS!** NOT **PAWS!**

WINK

WHERE ARE YOU FROM?
SNOTLAND!
SCOTLAND!
SCOTLAND.
HOW LONG ARE YOU VISITING?

ABOUT A HALF MOON.
TWO WEEKS! 'BOUT TWO WEEKS!

UH-HUH.

GOTTA WATCH THAT ONE.
YEAH. THAT'S LISA. YOU REMEMBER HER? SHE'S REALLY SMART. SHE FIGURED OUT HILO'S SECRET **ONCE** ALREADY.

BUT D. J. AND HILO CAST THAT SPELL YOU GAVE THEM AND ERASED THE MEMORIES OF THE WHOLE WORLD.
AYE.

THE **ORBS OF FELLBECK.** POWERFUL MEMORY CHARM.
TIME IS THE STONE THAT FALLS. TIME IS THE RIVER THAT CRAWLS.

AND IF THINGS GO BELLY-UP 'ROUND HERE WE COULD ALWAYS DO THAT DANCE AGAIN AND ERASE THE WORLD'S MEMORIES.

THANK YOU.
OUR PLEASURE.
AND IF WE'RE QUICK ABOUT THESE DISHES WE STILL MIGHT HAVE TIME TO VACUUM THE LIVING ROOM.

I THINK IT'S GOING REALLY WELL.

GOOD NIGHT! I WILL SEE YOU TOMORROW!

YEAH! OKAY! GOOD NIGHT! UM, BE -- CAREFUL!

CLACK

WELL, MOM, I AM GOING TO CHECK OVER MY HOMEWORK AND GET RIGHT TO BED!

YOU CERTAINLY ARE EFFICIENT TONIGHT.

GOOD NIGHT, MOM.
GOOD NIGHT.

D.J....

ARE YOU SURE YOU'RE OKAY?

ABSOLUTELY! I AM GOING TO GO BRUSH MY TEETH!

THIS IS BAD.
IT'LL BE FINE.

WE LEFT A **ROBOT** VERSION OF D. J. IN HIS HOUSE WITH HIS **FAMILY!**

AND IT'S **BRILLIANT** THAT YOU MADE AN ENTIRE ROBOT THAT IS ALMOST EXACTLY LIKE HIM, BUT...

HE'S KIND OF WHACK-A-DOO.

JUST ENOUGH WHACK-A-DOO THAT HIS FAMILY MIGHT NOTICE. IF THEY FIND OUT-- OH BOY.

YOU WOULD BE SURPRISED WHAT PEOPLE DON'T NOTICE.

WHAT?

SOMETIMES WHEN THE WEIRDEST OR MOST OBVIOUS THINGS ARE RIGHT IN FRONT OF THEM, PEOPLE DON'T SEE HOW WEIRD OR OBVIOUS THEY ARE.

PEOPLE LIKE TO THINK EVERYTHING IS GOING TO BE OKAY.

I'M WITH THE WEE LASS. I DON'T THINK THEY'LL SEE ANYTHING WRONG WITH D. J.
EVERYTHING IS GOING TO BE OKAY.

TWELVE MINUTES LATER.

SEVENTEEN MINUTES AND ONE EXPLANATION OF WHY D. J. IS A ROBOT LATER...

IZZY'S A ROBOT?
YES.
YEP.

HILO'S A ROBOT TOO?
YEP.
YES.

BUT HE'S NOT **THIS** ROBOT. HILO'S **ANOTHER** ROBOT, WHO IS WITH D. J. ON HIS HOME PLANET.
YES.

THIS IS SO AWESOME, I'M GONNA DIE!

I STILL LIKE HER. SHE'S SPUNKY.

AND YOU'RE A MAGICAL TALKING CAT!
AYE.

SO AWESOME!
AYE.

HOW'D YOU FIGURE OUT HE WASN'T D. J.?
LOTSA REASONS. BUT MOSTLY BECAUSE HE HASN'T TAKEN A PEE IN FIVE HOURS.
I TOTALLY HAVE NOT.

I FORGOT TO PROGRAM THEM TO PEE.

OKAY, BUT, LISA, NOW THAT YOU KNOW, YOU --
CAN'T TELL ANYBODY! I KNOW, **I KNOW!** MY PARENTS WOULD FREAK OUT. THEY'D CALL THE POLICE OR THE GOVERNMENT -- IT WOULD BE A DISASTER.
I MADE A MOUSE. IT CAN BAKE MUFFINS.

SO AWESOME!
SPUNK.

Y'SEE...

IT'S ALL WORKING OUT. SHE'LL SNEAK THEM HOME, COVER UP WHENEVER D. J. DOES ANY, Y'KNOW ...

WHACK-A-DOO-NESS.
AYE.

I GUESS. I JUST... I WANT TO **HELP** THEM. D. J. AND HILO ...

THEY'RE **NEVER** CAREFUL ENOUGH. **HILO** IS JUST THIS BIG BALL OF WILD ENERGY. AND **D. J.** WOULD THROW HIMSELF IN FRONT OF A **TRUCK** TO PROTECT HIM.

IT'S BETTER WHEN IT'S THREE OF YOU.
AYE.

YEAH. BUT THEY'RE ALL THE WAY ON ANOTHER PLANET. HOW CAN I DO ANYTHING IF I'M STUCK HERE?

YOU ARE HELPING THEM **RIGHT** NOW. KEEPING THEIR SECRET WHILE THEY'RE AWAY!

"FRIENDS WILL PROTECT YOUR EMPTY HOUSE." **THAT** IS WHAT THE ELDER SAID.

THE ELDER?

AYE! THE GREAT AND WISE TAMIR!

OH. I READ ABOUT HIM WHEN WE WERE ON YOUR WORLD. HE WAS THAT WARLORD WHO TOOK OVER ALL OF **OSHUN** A THOUSAND YEARS AGO.

**AYE!** HE WAS A **MONSTER!** A STORM OF DEATH AND RAGE! HE DEFEATED NEARLY **EVERY** CLAN ON THE PLANET!

THEN HE SET EVERYONE FREE.

YES. HE GAVE UP FIGHTING, BURIED HIS SWORD IN THE DIRT, AND SPENT THE REST OF HIS DAYS TEACHING LESSONS IN PEACE.

AND NO ONE EVER FOUND OUT WHY HE DECIDED TO BECOME GOOD.

NOPE. IT'S STILL A MYSTERY. BUT **NOW,** WITH THE SCALE TAIL CLAN ALL TOOTHLESS, THERE'S NO LONGER ANY WAR ON OSHUN.

WE DO HAVE TO PROTECT OURSELVES AND SCUTTLE IT UP A BIT WITH WARGIES AND POLLY-DOGGERS ...

BUT THAT ASIDE -- **EVERYONE** ON THE WHOLE TOPPING PLANET OF OSHUN LIVES PEACEFULLY NOW. WE FOLLOW THE **WAYS OF TAMIR.**

AND WHAT WOULD TAMIR TELL **ME?**
THAT YOU'RE A GOOD EGG WHO LOVES HER MATES.
EVERYTHING IS GOING TO BE DANDY.
CHEEP

# CHAPTER 7

## DANDY

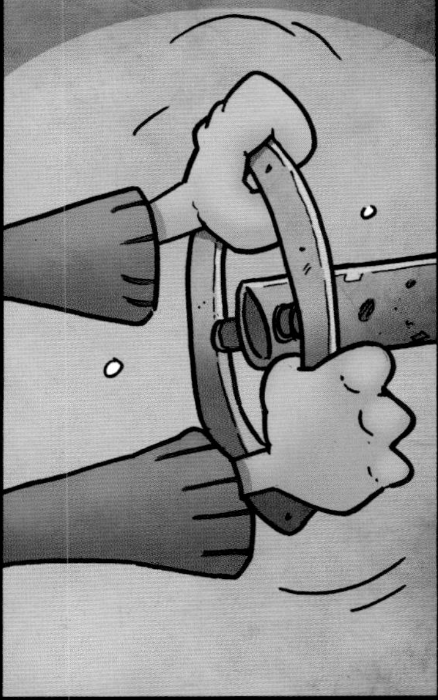

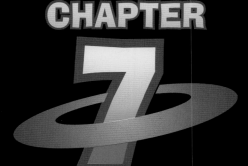

CRICK
TWEAK
TWEAK
TURN
TWEAK
CREEEEEEEK
UGH...
UGH...
SCRIIICK
SCRIIICK
SCRIIIIIICK
SCRIIICK
SCRIIICK

HEEEEEE

BINK

AAAH!
AAAH!

LOVE THAT GREETING! YOU OKAY?
YEAH. ARE YOU --

I'M OUTSTANDING! I FEEL POWERED UP!
YEAH. I UNCOVERED A WINDOW AND PULLED YOU INTO THE SUNLIGHT.

YOU UNCOVERED A WINDOW?!
I UNCOVERED A WINDOW.

RIGHT! YES! NOT JUST ANY WINDOW! DR. HORIZON INSTALLED GLASS THAT MAGNIFIES SOLAR RAYS.
SO I GOT TEN TIMES THE USUAL AMOUNT TO CHARGE ME UP!
I AM JUICED, BABY!
AND REMEMBERING STUFF!
YEAH. BUT NOT REMEMBERING IT ALL. WE --
AH RAH ROOOOOO
WHOA. WHAT WAS THAT?
I DIDN'T HEAR ANYTHING.
AH RAH RAH ROOOOOO
THAT! IT SOUNDS LIKE A BEAR TRYING TO BRUSH HIS TEETH.
AH RAH ROOOOO

HOLY MACKEREL! THAT'S YOUR STOMACH?! DUDE, YOU MUST BE STARVING.
KIND OF. I COULDN'T FIND ANY FOOD HERE. I DID FIND A TOILET.

AT LEAST I THINK IT WAS A TOILET. ALIEN BATHROOMS ARE WEIRD.

HANG ON. I CAN JUMPSTART THE WHOLE LAB NOW THAT MY GAS TANK IS FULL. I THINK THERE ARE SOME FOOD CONSTITUTORS IN HERE.
YOU WANNA DO THAT?

YOU KIND OF BLEW THE PLACE UP A BUNCH LAST NIGHT.

THAT'S WHEN I WAS ALL RUN-DOWN AND WOOGLY. I'M AT FULL CAPACITY NOW, BUBBA.
PINK

PLUNK
TZOOOOO

HOOOOM

BEEP

HILO.
YEAH.
SOMETHING'S BEEPING.
BEEP

SOUNDS LIKE A COUNTDOWN.
HILO.
BEEP

OH. IT **IS** A COUNTDOWN.
COUNTDOWN TO WHAT?!
BEEP

PRETTY SURE IT'S . . .

TO SELF-DESTRUCT.
**WHAT?!**

SO IT GOES
TOUGH COOKIES

BOOM

CRUNK

BWOOP

YOU OKAY?
YEAH. I'M -- AAH! HILO!

WHOOPS.

I'M GOING TO NEED THAT.

HOOOM

COOOOM

PLUK

ALL THE PIECES FIT.

HE PUT HIS ARM BACK ON.
HE'S A **ROBOT!**
-- CALLED HIM **HILO!**

IS THAT --
IT IS!
THAT'S HILO!

HE'S BACK!
HILO'S BACK!
HILO!

HEY!

HILO'S BACK!!

I'M BACK! TWO THINGS! ONE: I'M SORRY I DON'T REMEMBER YOU!

TWO: DOES ANYBODY HAVE ANY FOOD? D.J.'S HUNGRY!

THIS IS D.J.
HEY.

DID YOU COME BACK TO HELP US?
NOTHING WORKS. ALL OUR POWER IS GONE.
PLEASE! YOU HAVE TO BRING IT BACK!

OKAY! OKAY! I'LL DO WHAT I CAN, BUT I NEED TO FIND OUT --
WAS IT **RAZORWARK?!**
OF COURSE IT WAS RAZORWARK!

HE DESTROYED **FARALON,** THEN HE LEFT US TO DIE!
YOU'VE COME BACK TO SAVE US!
**PLEASE!**

**I WILL!**
WHAT IS THAT?

WE CAN'T LIVE LIKE THIS!
WE NEED YOU!
**I'LL HELP!**
IT'S TOO SUNNY. I CAN'T SEE . . .

RAZORWARK DID IT!
PLEASE BRING THE POWER BACK!
NOTHING WORKS!
I'LL TRY!
WHOA.

I HAVE TO FIND OUT WHAT HAPPENED!
PLEASE!
HILO!

I PROMISE I WILL --
HILO!

D.J.?

D.J.!
D.J.!

# CHAPTER 8

# PERMANENT RECORD

AAH!
I LOVE THAT GREETING!
I'D LOVE TO! BUT I'VE GOT PILES TO DO HERE! AND I'M GETTING READY TO BARBECUE!

YOU'RE GETTING BETTER.

ALL THE PIECES FIT.

AAH!
AAH!

I LOVE THAT GREETING.

THE LIM HOUSE.
HAVE A GOOD DAY, JENNIFER.
YOU TOO, MOM.

MOTHER, I HOPE YOUR DAY IS EVENTFUL AND JOYOUS.
OKAY! **STILL** SO POLITE THIS MORNING, D.J.
YEAH! I LIKE IT!

I DO --
TOO.

DO YOU ... DO YOU THINK D.J.'S ALL RIGHT?
SURE. WHY?

HE . . . IT SEEMS SO SILLY, I DON'T EVEN KNOW WHY I'M. . . BUT. . .

HIS HUG SEEMED DIFFERENT.

SORRY?
NOTHING. NEVER MIND.

I'M SURE IT'S NOTHING.

LET'S BE POLITE AND WELCOMING TO HILO AND IZZY'S FRIEND --
VANDERBILT ELEMENTARY SCHOOL

POLLY KORIMAKO.
SHE WILL BE JOINING OUR CLASS WHILE SHE VISITS THEM.
OI!

AND POLLY, WHERE ARE YOU VISITING FROM?
SOCKLAND!
SCOTLAND!
SCOTLAND!

ARE YOU ENJOYING YOUR STAY HERE IN AMERICA?

OH YES. YOU ALL SMELL WEIRD, AND YOUR FOOD IS AWFUL.

KING

HOW IS THAT RUDE? YOU **DO** SMELL BAD. CAT NOSES CAN TELL.

AND YOUR VITTLES -- **BLECH.** IT'S A MIRACLE I'M NOT BARFING FIVE TIMES A DAY.
POLLY...

THE **PLAN** IS THAT YOU'RE GOING TO HELP ME BY MAKING SURE FAKE HILO AND D.J. DON'T ATTRACT TOO MUCH ATTENTION.

THAT MEANS **YOU** CAN'T ATTRACT TOO MUCH ATTENTION.
UNDERSTOOD. YOU'LL BE SHOCKED HOW THIS **CAT** CAN BE AS QUIET AS A **MOUSE.**

A SINGLE **HONEYBEE** WILL VISIT FIFTY TO ONE HUNDRED FLOWERS ON JUST ONE TRIP OUT OF THE HIVE.

UNLESS IT'S A **HIPPO BEE.**

EXCUSE ME?

IF IT'S A **WEE** BEE, THEN IT GOES BACK TO ITS HIVE ALL THE TIME. IF IT'S A HIPPOPOTAMUS BEE --
STOP.

WELL, THEY WEIGH THREE TONS AND CARRY TWENTY GALLONS OF NECTAR IN THEIR POUCHES.

**WHICH** ARE ATTACHED TO THEIR RATHER GIGANTIC BUTTS.

AT LEAST THEY DO IN **SOCKLAND!**
SNOTLAND.
D. J. AND I HAVE MADE MODELS OF WHAT THE HIPPO BEES MIGHT LOOK LIKE!
ARE THE BUTTS BIG ENOUGH?

HOW WAS I TO KNOW THAT YOU'VE GOT DIFFERENT CREATURES HERE?
**YOU** WERE GOING TO STAY QUIET!

I **WAS!** I DIDN'T DEMONSTRATE THE SOUND OF THE HIPPO BEE **MATING CALL!**

BLAAAAAAP

THAT WOULD HAVE ATTRACTED ATTENTION!

YOU'RE A TOTAL WEIRDO.
THANK YOU!

IT'S NOT A GOOD THING, DUMMY.
NO?

NO. DO THEY THINK WEIRDO IS GOOD WHERE YOU COME FROM? DO --

AAAH!
ATTA BOY! FIGHT BACK! MAKE YOUR FAMILY PROUD!

PRINCIPAL'S OFFICE
I DIDN'T KNOW YOU DON'T FIGHT AT SCHOOL! AT MY SCHOOL, ALL WE DO IS FIGHT!
PRINCIPAL'S OFFICE
PRINCIPAL'S OFFICE
DO YOU EVER HIT EACH OTHER WITH STICKS?
NO.
PRINCIPAL'S OFFICE

HEY, BILLY IS OUR FRIEND!
**YEAH.** YOU FIGHT HIM, YOU GOTTA FIGHT **US.**
I WON'T BE FIGHTING ANYONE.

SAYS YOU.
SHOVE

SORRY. I FORGOT TO TAKE OUT FAKE HILO'S AND D. J.'S PROTECTION PROGRAMS. THEY WON'T LET ANY OF US GET HURT.
WE WILL NOT!
NOPE.
PRINCIPAL'S OFFICE

MY FOOD SMELLS GROSS?! YOU SHOULD TAKE A WHIFF OF THAT SLOP YOU CALL A MEAL WITH MY SNORTER! YOU'LL HORK UP AN OCEAN, LADDIE.

PRINICPAL'S OFFICE.
YOU ARE ALL THIS FAR AWAY FROM HAVING A REPORT IN YOUR PERMANENT RECORDS!
OUTSTANDING!
SO NOT OUTSTANDING.

LTON
KING

KING

MY BAD. I CAN'T STAND HAIR PULLING.

SORRY. I THOUGHT IT WAS MY TURN.

PRINCIPAL'S OFFICE
THAT'S IT!

ALL OF THIS IS GOING ON YOUR **PERMANENT RECORDS.**

THIS WILL FOLLOW YOU TO YOUR HIGH SCHOOLS AND COLLEGES.
LUCKY FOR ME I LIVE ON ANOTHER PLANET.

EVERYONE IS GOING TO KNOW WHAT YOU DID.

TYPE
TYPE
TYPE

GINA COOPER
VANDERBILT ELEMENTARY

DANIEL JACKSON LIM
VANDERBILT ELEMENTARY

ISABELLA

HILO

SECTOR E.
THESE ARE **WHO?**

**POSSIBLE** MATCHES FOR **THE COMET.**

THE COMPUTERS HAVE FOUND THAT THEY'RE IN THE FIFTY TO SIXTY PERCENT RANGE OF MATCHING.
UH-HUH.

WHY IS THERE A DOG?

FIFTY-ONE PERCENT MATCH.
WE'RE **SO** GOING TO THE SOUTH POLE.

BEEP
MATCH
SIR?
MATCH

CONFIRMED MATCH! SIR! WE HAVE A CONFIRMED MATCH!
MATCH

ONE HUNDRED PERCENT MATCH. THIS **IS** THE COMET!
MATCH

WHERE?
SIR?

WHERE. IS. HE?

# BLOODMOON AND LIGHT

OKAY, BIG BIRD.

DROP HIM.

WHU?
SQUAWK
GOTCHA!
THAT'S A **BIG** BIRD!
I KNOW, RIGHT?!
SNAP
WHOA.
WHOA!

SCRAAACK
HOOF

HILO.
I SEE 'EM!

GIANT RAT PROBLEM!

STOP!

YOU HAD **ONE** JOB AND YOU GRAB THE WRONG BOY. STUPID MACHINES.

HELLO, HILO.
YOU'RE... YOU'RE **DR. BLOODMOON.**
I AM.
IT'S SO GOOD TO SEE YOU AGAIN.

SO...

YOU DON'T REMEMBER ME.
I REMEMBER YOU A LITTLE...

I REMEMBER THAT YOU CREATED **RAZORWARK.**

AND THAT **YOU** SENT HIM TO FIGHT WARS.

THAT ISN'T WHAT HAPPENED. YOU, D.J., HAVE BEEN MISINFORMED.

AND YOU, HILO...

YOUR MEMORIES HAVE BEEN ERASED.

WHAT IS THE LAST THING YOU REMEMBER BEFORE LEAVING **JANNUS?**

RAZORWARK DESTROYED FARALON. I FOUGHT HIM. WE FOUGHT SO HARD WE RIPPED A HOLE -- A PORTAL -- INTO THE VOID... AND I GOT SCARED.

BOOM
I RAN AWAY. I FLEW INTO THE VOID. THEN I LANDED ON EARTH.

RAZORWARK FOLLOWED YOU INTO THE VOID. THAT'S THE LAST THIS WORLD HAS SEEN OF EITHER OF YOU.

WHAT HAPPENED HERE? WHY IS THERE NO POWER? WHY DON'T MACHINES WORK?

EXCEPT HERS.

THESE ARE YOUR ROBOTS, RIGHT?

YES. MY MACHINES STILL WORK.

LET ME TELL YOU WHAT YOU HAVE FORGOTTEN.

I AM **CONSTANCE BLOODMOON,** THE LEADING ROBOTIC SCIENTIST IN THE WORLD.

I SPENT **YEARS** MAKING EXTRAORDINARY ROBOTS. BUT I **KNEW** I COULD MAKE ONE THAT WAS BETTER.

I WANTED TO CREATE ONE THAT DIDN'T JUST DRIVE A CAR OR SERVE FOOD OR CLEAN A HOUSE.

YES. MY ROBOTS HAD LIMITED EMOTIONS. I COULDN'T MAKE THEM **FEEL.**

HOW DID YOU FINALLY DO IT?
I GOT HELP.

A TRAVELER FROM ANOTHER WORLD CAME TO VISIT ME.

HE WAS A BIG TALKING **CAT.**

WHAT?

HIS NAME WAS **TAMIR.**

TAMIR EXPLAINED TO ME THAT HE TRAVELED THROUGH A DIMENSIONAL PORTAL. HE CALLED IT A **DOOR.**
ON MY WORLD WE CALL A DOOR LIKE THAT **MAGIC.** HERE YOU CALL IT **SCIENCE.** IT IS MOSTLY THE SAME.
HE EXPLAINED TO ME THAT HE USED TO BE A FIERCE WARRIOR.
I WAS A CREATURE OF RAGE AND GREED. I SOUGHT ONLY TO HURT AND TO CONQUER AND TO **RULE** MY WORLD.
AND I DID.
UNTIL I FOUND **THIS.**

MY ARMY HAD JUST DEFEATED THE WILLOW TRIBE OF MOUNT FATUM. THEY WERE A RESILIENT BUT ULTIMATELY SIMPLE PEOPLE.

THEY MOSTLY DWELLED WITHIN THEIR MOUNTAIN, WHICH SHOULD'VE BEEN **FAR** TOO COLD TO LIVE IN.

BUT WHEN WE VENTURED IN, WE WERE BATHED IN SUCH WARMTH. SUCH A COMFORTING HEAT.

I ALONE SEARCHED FOR THE SOURCE OF THIS HEAT, AND WHEN I FOUND IT...
I DISCOVERED SO MUCH **MORE** THAN A SOLUTION TO THE COLD.

WHAT?
LOVE.
I'M SORRY?
FOR THE FIRST TIME IN MY LIFE . . .
I EXPERIENCED THE FEELING OF LOVE.
I WAS BORN ENSLAVED, BEATEN, STARVED, ABUSED, AND FORCED TO WORK UNTIL THE DAY I WAS STRONG ENOUGH TO FIGHT BACK.
I NEVER FELT LOVED OR LOVED ANYTHING.
THEN I SAW THIS LIGHT.

AND YOU FELL IN LOVE WITH IT?

NO.

AGAIN, IN MY WORLD, WE CALL IT MAGIC. YOU WOULD CALL IT SCIENCE.

I KNOW HOW THE MIND WORKS. I KNOW HOW THE BRAIN WORKS . . .

SOME PARTS OF THE BRAIN ARE USED TO MAKE OUR LIMBS MOVE. SOME PARTS OF THE BRAIN HELP US SPEAK.

AND ONE PART OF THE BRAIN IS USED FOR --
EMOTION.
YES.

THE ROCK IS **MAGIC.** IT IS A POWERFUL SOURCE OF ENERGY, BUT IT **ALSO** TOUCHES THE PART OF A LIVING BRAIN THAT ALLOWS US TO **FEEL.**

I FELT **LOVE.**
AND LOVE IS ALL THAT I TEACH.

BUT I WANT **YOU** TO HAVE IT.

WHY?
MY WORLD IS STILL VERY ... **DANGEROUS.** LIKE I USED TO BE. FILLED WITH RAGE AND GREED.

CREATURES WITH EVIL IN THEIR HEART COULD USE IT TO DESTROY EVERYTHING.

A POWER LIKE THIS COULD RAIN DOWN ON US ALL.

HE SAID SORCERERS ON HIS WORLD WHO COULD SEE THE FUTURE TOLD HIM TO COME TO JANNUS AND GIVE IT TO ME.
HE CALLED IT **EMPATIS.**

AND IT WAS THE **MOST** POWERFUL ENERGY SOURCE I HAD EVER SEEN.

BUT MORE IMPORTANT . . .
IT BROUGHT **RAZORWARK** TO LIFE.
HE WAS THOUGHTFUL.
HE WAS FUNNY.
HE WAS KIND.
HE WAS **ALIVE.**
AND I SENT HIM OUT INTO THE WORLD TO BE ITS CHAMPION.

OUR WORLD'S HERO.

BUT YOU MADE HIM FIGHT YOUR ENEMIES. AND HE TURNED AGAINST YOU.

SENDING HIM TO FIGHT WAS **NOT** MY DECISION.

AND HE DIDN'T GO TO WAR WITH US BECAUSE WE MADE HIM FIGHT.

WE DID SOMETHING MUCH WORSE.

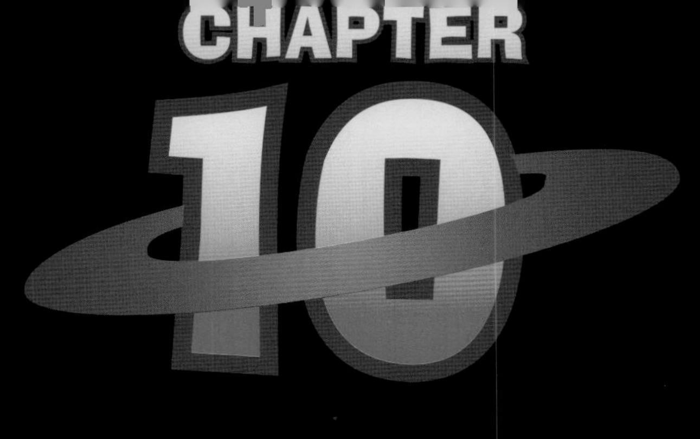

# CHAPTER 10

# THEN EVERYTHING WENT WRONG

HOW COULD YOU LET THIS HAPPEN?!
I DIDN'T LET IT HAPPEN! IT JUST -- Y'KNOW -- HAPPENED!

FIGHTING? ARE YOU SURE THIS IS ACTUALLY D.J.?

THIS IS ACTUALLY D.J.!!

MAN, YOU'RE GOING TO BE GROUNDED UNTIL YOU'RE THIRTY.
WATCH IT, DUDE. D.J. MIGHT BEAT YOU UP.

I'D LIKE TO SEE HIM TRY.

GIVE ME A BREAK, DEXTER. LISA COULD BEAT YOU UP.
TOTALLY.

IN MY HOUSE WE'D BE HITTING EACH OTHER WITH STICKS BY NOW.

YOU THREE NEED TO GO HOME. **NOW.** GINA, YOUR MOTHER IS WAITING FOR YOU. IZZY, HILO -- YOUR **UNCLE TROUT,** WELL, HE KEEPS TALKING ABOUT BARBECUE, BUT YOU SHOULD GO HOME.

SIGH.

I AM JUST SO DISAPPOINTED IN **ALL** OF YOU.

YOU HAVE MY DEEPEST APOLOGIES, MOTHER. IT WAS NEVER MY INTENTION TO CAUSE YOU EMOTIONAL DISCOMFORT.

DANIEL.
WHAT'S WRONG?
NOTHING AT ALL, MOM.

NO. WHY ARE YOU BEING SO FORMAL? AND WHY DID YOU GET INTO FIGHTS TODAY? WHAT HAPPENED?

THIS ISN'T YOU.

IT'S GOING TO BE OKAY, MRS. LIM. YOU'LL SEE.

I'LL SEE?

THINGS COME TOGETHER. LIKE GINA, HILO, AND D. J. I KNOW IT SEEMS WEIRD... BUT I PROMISE...

THE PIECES WILL FIT.

IZZY, I DON'T KNOW WHAT YOU MEAN.
MOM?

OH. I HAVE TO GO.
BEEP
MOM.

IN A MINUTE, SWEETHEART. IZZY, HOW ARE HILO, GINA, AND D.J. **TOGETHER?**

MOM.

HANG ON! IZZY, HOW ARE --

WAIT, WHERE'D IZZY GO?
I DON'T KNOW. SHE WAS --

MOM!

WHAT?

I THINK THE **GOVERNMENT** IS ON THE FRONT LAWN.

AAH!
WE'RE GOING TO NEED PLENTY OF STICKS.

YOU HAVE TO KNOW IT WASN'T MY IDEA TO SEND RAZORWORK TO FIGHT OUR WARS. I **BEGGED** OUR GOVERNMENT NOT TO. THEN I BEGGED THEM TO **STOP.**

THEN RAZORWARK ASKED TO STOP.
I DON'T WANT TO DO IT ANYMORE.

I KNOW.

THEY MAKE ME FIGHT ROBOTS.

I KNOW.

THEY MAKE ME **DESTROY** ROBOTS.

THESE ARE ROBOTS THAT ARE **ONLY** DOING WHAT THEY'VE BEEN **PROGRAMMED** TO DO.

THEY DON'T HAVE **EMOTIONS** LIKE ME. THEY DON'T **FEEL** THINGS AS DEEPLY AS ME...

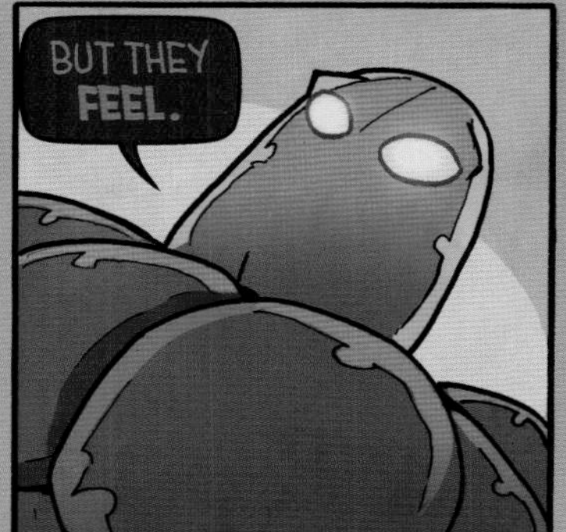
BUT THEY
**FEEL.**

AND BEFORE I **DESTROY** THEM ...
WHEN THEY **SEE** ME ...
WHEN THEY **KNOW** WHAT WILL HAPPEN ...

THEY'RE **SO** AFRAID.

I'M NOT DOING
IT ANYMORE.

NO MORE
FIGHTING.

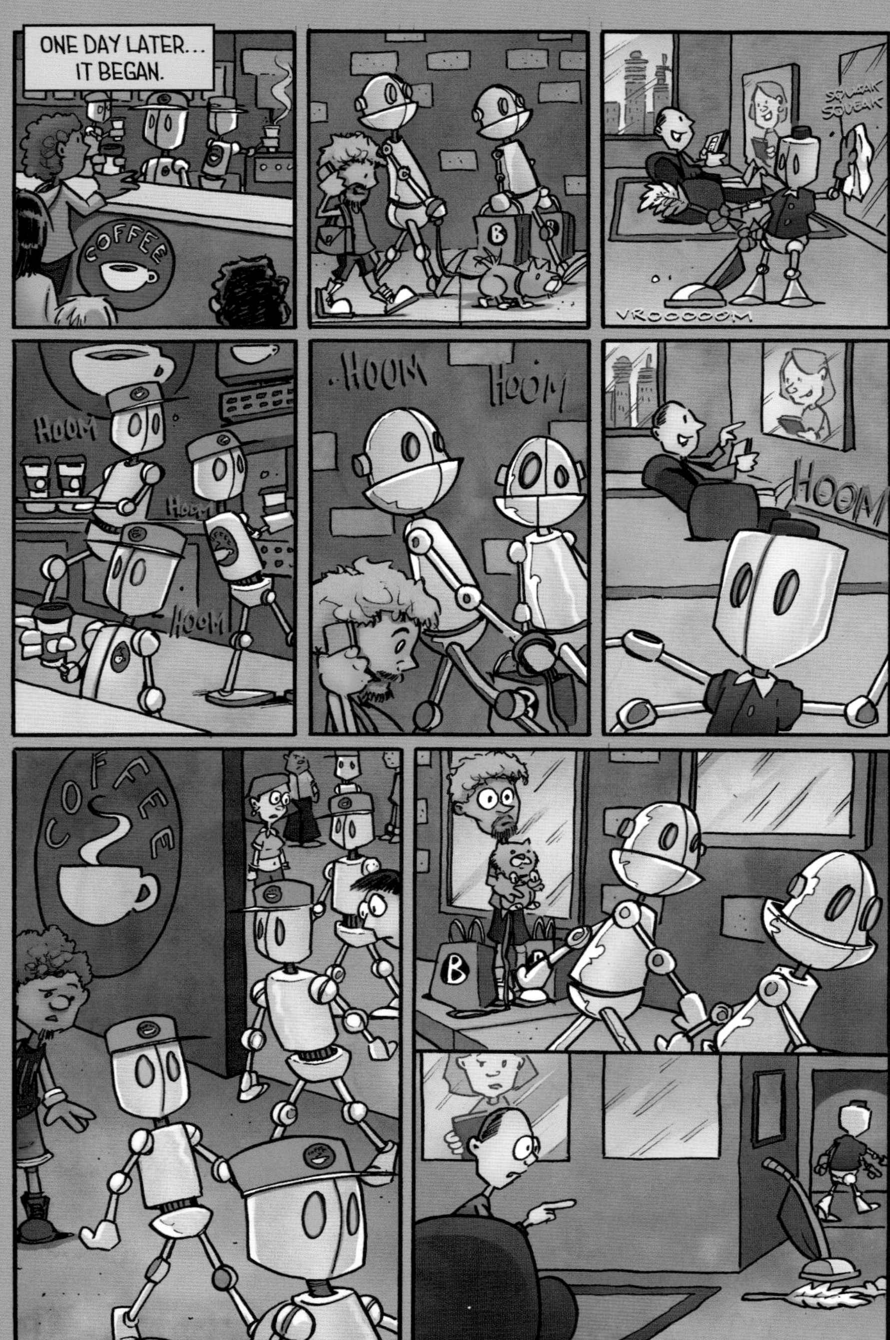
ONE DAY LATER... IT BEGAN.
COFFEE
SQUEAK SQUEAK
VROOOOOOM
HOOM
HOOM
HOOM
HOOM
HOOM
HOOM
COFFEE

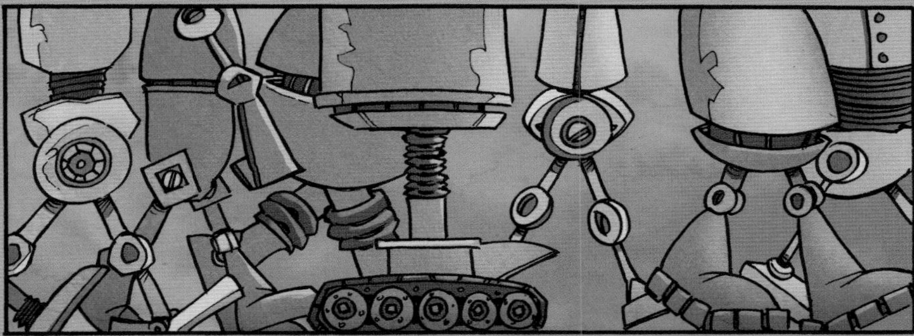

HOW MANY ROBOTS
HAVE LEFT?

HE SENT A MESSAGE!

WHO?

RAZORWARK.

I AM SETTING THEM FREE.

ALL OF THESE ROBOTS WILL JOIN ME IN THE GREAT WESTERN DESERT.
WE **NEED** NOTHING FROM YOU.
WE **WANT** NOTHING FROM YOU EXCEPT... TO BE LEFT ALONE.
WE WILL BUILD A LIFE AWAY FROM YOU.
AWAY FROM ALL OF YOU.
AWAY FROM ALL OF YOU
AWAY FROM ALL OF YOU
WE WILL BUILD OUR LIFE TOGETHER
WE WILL BUILD OUR LIFE TOGETHER
WE WILL BUILD OUR LIFE TOGETHER

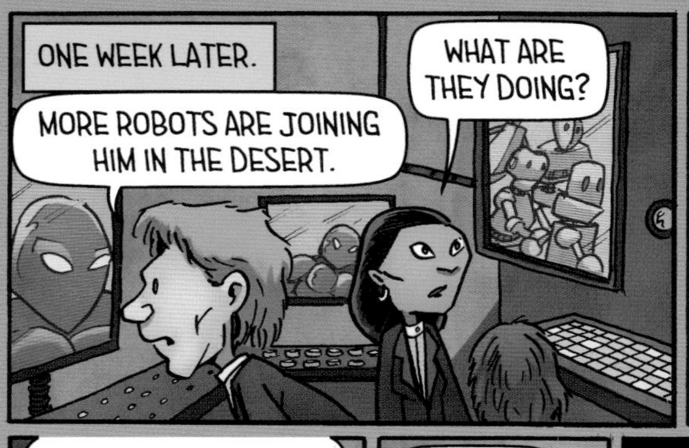
ONE WEEK LATER.
MORE ROBOTS ARE JOINING HIM IN THE DESERT.
WHAT ARE THEY DOING?

BUILDING HOUSES FOR THEMSELVES.

HAS HE TAKEN **ALL** THE ROBOTS IN THE ENTIRE WORLD?

NOT YET.

AS THE WEEKS WENT ON, LEADERS OF THE WORLD'S NATIONS GATHERED . . .

THEY SAID THEY WERE **ANGRY** THAT THE ROBOTS WEREN'T DOING THEIR WORK ANYMORE . . .

BUT THAT WASN'T THE WHOLE TRUTH.
THEY WERE **SCARED**.

YOU CANNOT DO THIS! IT'S **WRONG!** THEY HAVEN'T DONE **ANYTHING!**

**YET,** DR. BLOODMOON. THEY HAVEN'T DONE ANYTHING **YET.**

THEY DON'T NEED **FOOD.** THEY DON'T NEED **CLOTHING.** THEY DON'T EXPERIENCE **FEAR.**

THEY COULD BE THE PERFECT ARMY.
IF RAZORWARK DECIDES TO ATTACK THE WORLD WITH HIS RACE OF ROBOTS . . .
THEY COULD DESTROY US ALL.

HE WON'T DO THAT.

IT'S NOT A CHANCE WE CAN TAKE.

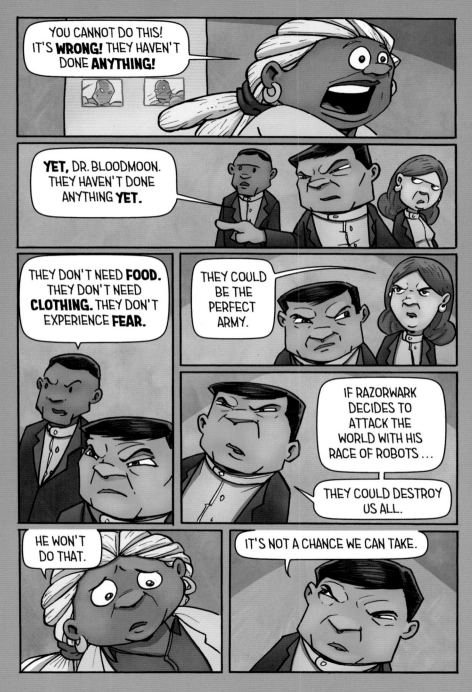

IT WAS SIMPLY CALLED **THE MASTER SWITCH.**

AND IT WAS CREATED IN CASE THE ROBOTS EVER TURNED AGAINST US.

WHAT DID IT DO?

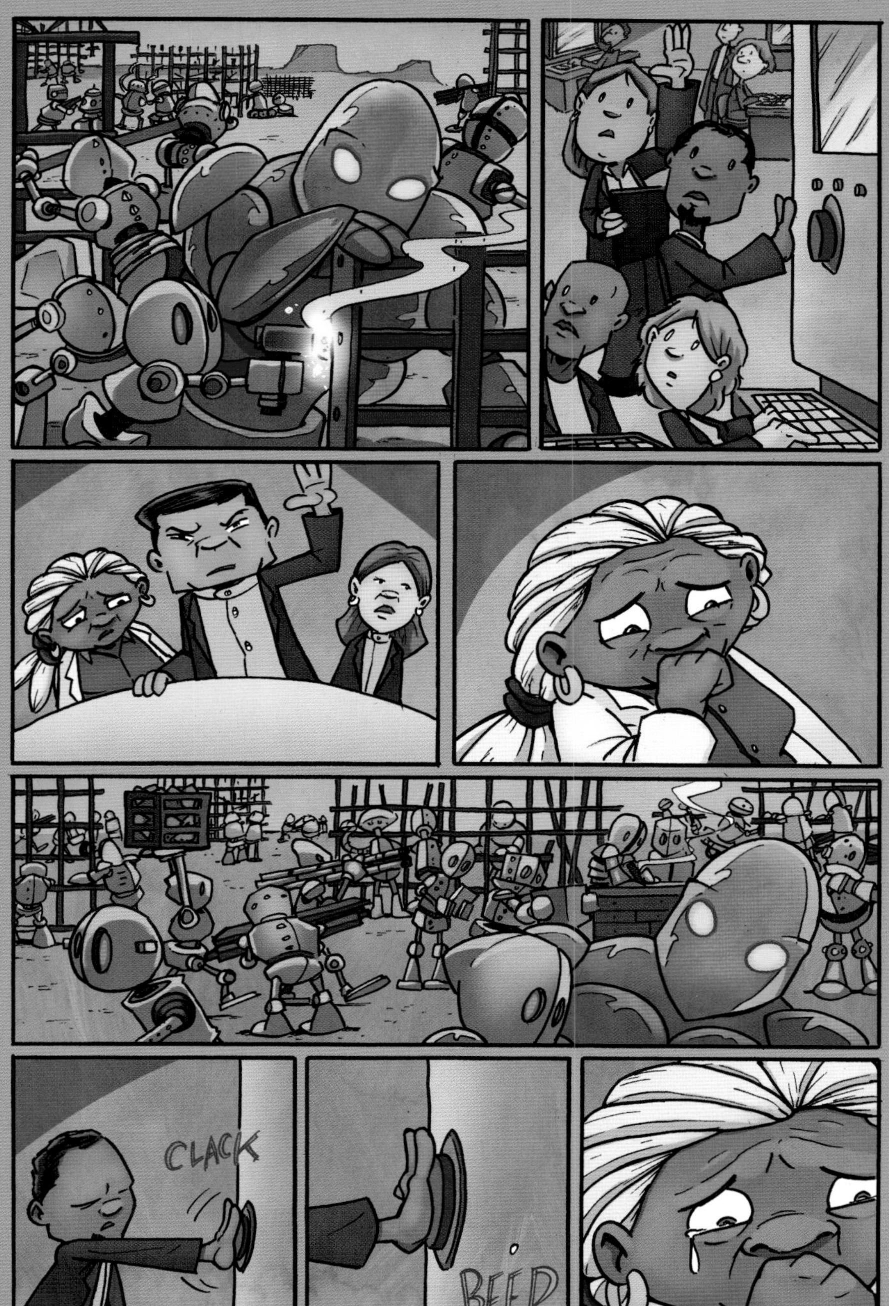
CLACK
BEEP

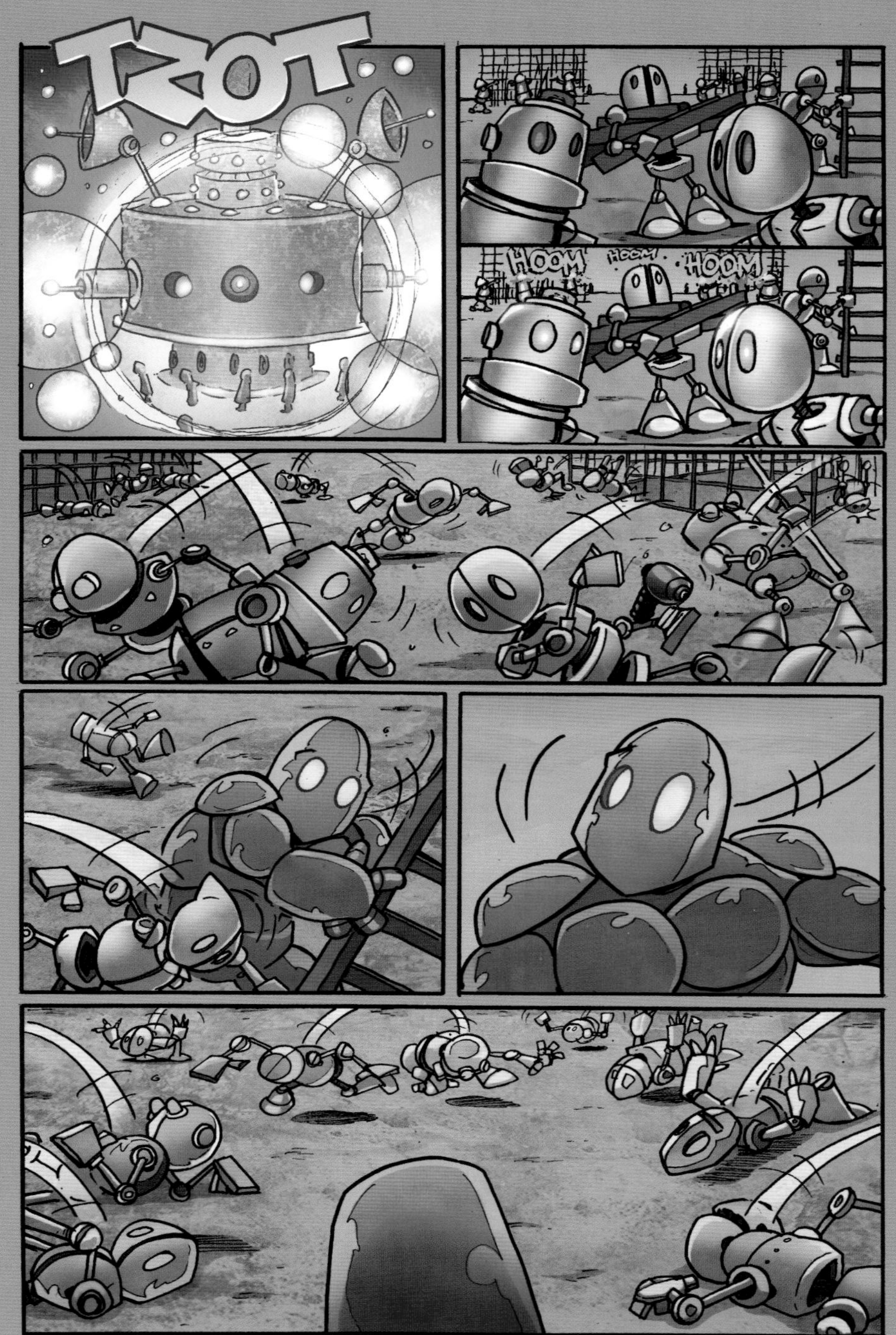
TZOT
HOOM
HOOM
HOOM

THE MASTER SWITCH
SHUT OFF ALL THE ROBOTS.

EXCEPT RAZORWARK.
HE WAS **SO**...
BROKEN.
YES.
BROKEN.

HE DESTROYED **SEVEN** ROBOT FACTORIES IN ONE DAY.

HIS MESSAGE WAS CLEAR.

THAT WAS WHY HE WENT TO WAR WITH US.

WHY DID YOU LET THEM DO THAT?

WHAT?

WHY DID YOU LET THEM? YOU MADE HIM TO SAVE PEOPLE. AND THEN YOU LET THEM TURN HIM INTO A WEAPON.

I TRIED TO STOP THEM.

YOU SHOULD HAVE TRIED HARDER!

THAT'S YOUR JOB! HE PROTECTED THE WORLD, AND YOU WERE SUPPOSED TO PROTECT HIM!

I KNOW.

AND THEN YOU LET THEM KILL ALL OF HIS FRIENDS!!

YOU LET THEM MAKE HIM INTO A MONSTER!

**I KNOW!!**

AND THEY ARE BEING **PUNISHED** FOR IT! DON'T YOU SEE?!

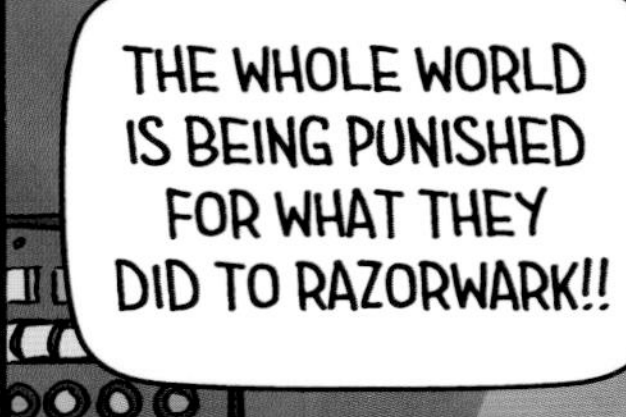

THE WHOLE WORLD IS BEING PUNISHED FOR WHAT THEY DID TO RAZORWARK!!

ALL THE ENERGY IS GONE! NO MORE MACHINES TO DO THEIR WORK! TO LIVE THEIR LIVES! **TO FIGHT THEIR WARS!**
THEY HAVE TO START OVER! **THEY ARE BEING PUNISHED FOR WHAT THEY DID!**

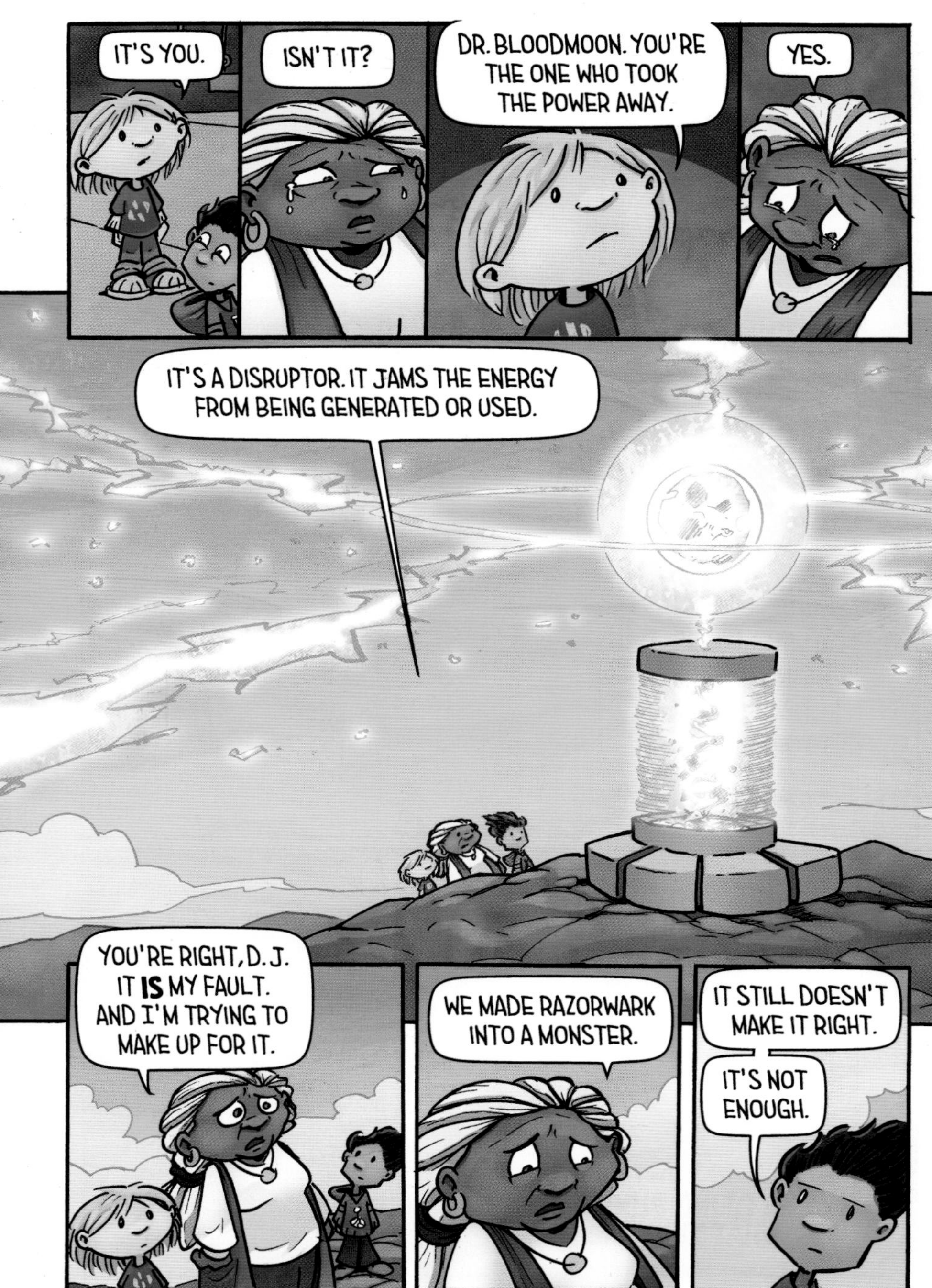
IT'S YOU.
ISN'T IT?
DR. BLOODMOON. YOU'RE THE ONE WHO TOOK THE POWER AWAY.
YES.
IT'S A DISRUPTOR. IT JAMS THE ENERGY FROM BEING GENERATED OR USED.
YOU'RE RIGHT, D. J. IT **IS** MY FAULT. AND I'M TRYING TO MAKE UP FOR IT.
WE MADE RAZORWARK INTO A MONSTER.
IT STILL DOESN'T MAKE IT RIGHT.
IT'S NOT ENOUGH.

NO.

BUT IT'S HARD TO PROTECT PEOPLE WE LOVE FROM TERRIBLE THINGS.

IT'S HARD TO SAVE THEM.

STILL . . . WHAT WE DO WHEN TERRIBLE THINGS HAPPEN TO **US** . . .

**THAT** SHOWS WHO WE ARE.

RAZORWARK BECAME A MONSTER.

THEN HE WANTED US TO DO WRONG.

THAT'S NOT WHO WE ARE.

WE?

YES. ME AND IZZY.

WHAT DO YOU KNOW ABOUT IZZY?

# CHAPTER 11

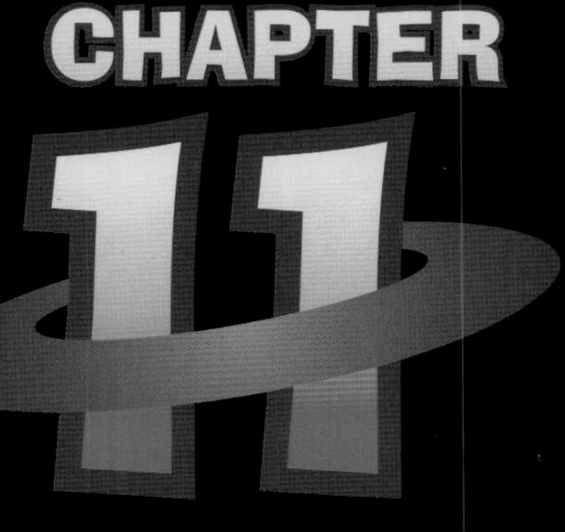

H

GOOD DAY TO YOU ALL.
I AM **SECTOR E** DIRECTOR TILLER. AND BY ORDER OF THE FEDERAL GOVERNMENT, WE WILL BE TAKING THE BOY KNOWN AS **THE COMET** -- ALSO KNOWN AS **HILO** -- INTO CUSTODY.

THEY THINK HILO IS **THE COMET?!**
WHAT'S **SECTOR E?**

GINA?
STAY CALM.

WHAT ARE YOU TALKING ABOUT? THIS BOY ISN'T THE COMET. THAT'S JUST CRAZY.
THAT IS CORRECT. I AM NOT THE COMET.
HE IS NOT.

**DO YOU HAVE A WARRANT?!**
**MOM, CALL A LAWYER!**

WAIT, HANG ON, WE SHOULD GET UNCLE TROUT. HE'S HILO'S GUARDIAN. I'M SURE --

WE HAVE "UNCLE TROUT" IN CUSTODY.
HE'S NOT SO MUCH AN **UNCLE** AS HE IS AN **ANDROID.**
AND I'M GETTING READY TO BARBECUE!

GINA.
STAY CALM.

ENOUGH! HE'S COMING WITH US NOW. **TAKE HIM.**

**YOU'RE** NOT TAKING HIM **ANYWHERE!**

HOW DO WE EVEN KNOW YOU'RE FROM THE GOVERNMENT?!
YEAH!

**TAKE HIM NOW.**

**STAND ASIDE, PLEASE!**
**DON'T TOUCH HER!**

STAND ASIDE!

NO!

NOW!

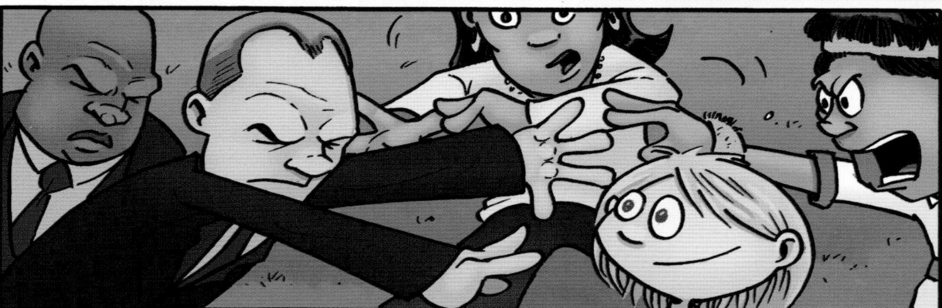

TZAACK

WHOOPS.

DO I STILL HAVE
TO STAY CALM?

DO YOU MEAN **IZZY'S** ON **EARTH?**
YES. SHE'S FINE. DR. HORIZON IS THERE TOO. HE'S UNCONSCIOUS, BUT --
DID YOU SAY **HORIZON?**
YES. HE CAME THROUGH THE VOID TO HELP US.
WHAT'S WRONG?
SO MANY THINGS.
HILO... I THINK RAZORWARK DIDN'T JUST **BLOCK OUT** YOUR MEMORIES.
I THINK HE **CHANGED** MANY OF THEM.

CHANGED MY MEMORIES?

YES. I THINK MANY THINGS YOU REMEMBER MIGHT NOT BE TRUE.

TELL ME WHAT YOU KNOW ABOUT IZZY?

SHE'S MY SISTER. RAZORWARK MADE HER TO CREATE **WEAPONS.** SHE WOULDN'T DO IT. HE WAS GOING TO **DEACTIVATE** HER...

I TOOK HER, AND WE RAN AWAY TO LIVE WITH DR. HORIZON.

NO. YOU DIDN'T. **THINK.**
YOUR MEMORIES ARE COMING BACK ... **THINK.** TRY TO SEE THAT DAY YOU ESCAPED WITH IZZY.
SEE IT.
BOOM
BOOM

YOU **DIDN'T** RUN AWAY TO LIVE WITH DR. HORIZON.

I **DID.**

**NO.**

NO.

WE CAME TO LIVE WITH YOU.

YES.

**WHY**... WHY DID RAZORWARK WANT US TO THINK WE LIVED WITH **DR. HORIZON?**

HILO. MY ROBOTICS **PROJECT** WAS CALLED RAZORWARK. THAT'S WHY THE **WORLD** CALLED HIM THAT.

BUT I HAD A **DIFFERENT** NAME FOR HIM. I TOLD YOU. DO YOU REMEMBER?
A
B

IT TOOK **EIGHT** TRIES TO MAKE HIM.
D
F
G
H

JUST LIKE YOU.
H

I . . . REMEMBER.

HILO? WHAT IS IT? WHAT DO YOU REMEMBER?

**HIS NAME.**

HILO'S HOUSE.

YOU'RE READY.
BEEP

TSSSST

SHOOoOOOOM

HELLO, IZZY.

HELLO.
YOU REPAIRED MUCH QUICKER THAN I THOUGHT YOU WOULD.
HOW ARE YOU FEELING?

I AM OUTSTANDING.

HILO...IZZY WENT BACK TO HIM.
SHE LEFT **US** AND WENT BACK TO **HIM.**

NO. SHE... **NO.**
**NO.**

THANK YOU, IZZY. YOU **ALWAYS** FIXED WHAT'S BROKEN.

HILO! WHAT IS IT?!

I REMEMBER RAZORWARK'S NAME.

HORIZON.

# END OF BOOK FIVE

"An action-packed page-turner with heart!"
—DAV PILKEY, author of the DOG MAN series
NEW YORK TIMES BESTSELLING SERIES
HILO
ALL THE PIECES FIT
BY
JUDD
WINICK

**JUDD WINICK** is the creator of the award-winning, **New York Times** bestselling Hilo series. Judd grew up on Long Island with a healthy diet of doodling, **X-Men** comics, the newspaper strip **Bloom County**, and **Looney Tunes**. Today, he lives in San Francisco with his wife, Pam Ling; their two kids; their cat, Chaka; and far too many action figures and vinyl toys for a normal adult. Judd created the Cartoon Network series **Juniper Lee**; has written issues of superhero comics, including Batman, Green Lantern, and Green Arrow; and was a cast member of MTV's **The Real World: San Francisco**. Judd is also the author of the highly acclaimed graphic novel **Pedro and Me**, about his **Real World** roommate and friend, AIDS activist Pedro Zamora. Visit Judd and Hilo online at juddspillowfort.com or find him on Twitter at @JuddWinick.